Shannon,

Thanks for reading!

Sawyer Bennett

Wicked Wish

(The Wicked Horse Vegas Series)

By
Sawyer Bennett

All Rights Reserved.

Copyright © 2017 by Sawyer Bennett

Published by Big Dog Books

This book is a work of fiction. Names, characters, places, and incidents either are products of the author's imagination or are used fictiously. Any resemblance to actual events, locales or persons, living or dead, is entirely coincidental.

No part of this book can be reproduced in any form or by electronic or mechanical means including information storage and retrieval systems, without the express written permission of the author. The only exception is by a reviewer who may quote short excerpts in a review.

ISBN: 978-1-940883-81-6

Find Sawyer on the web!
sawyerbennett.com
twitter.com/bennettbooks
facebook.com/bennettbooks

Table of Contents

Foreword	v
CHAPTER 1	1
CHAPTER 2	9
CHAPTER 3	21
CHAPTER 4	31
CHAPTER 5	40
CHAPTER 6	52
CHAPTER 7	64
CHAPTER 8	73
CHAPTER 9	83
CHAPTER 10	92
CHAPTER 11	102
CHAPTER 12	113
CHAPTER 13	122
CHAPTER 14	133
CHAPTER 15	146
CHAPTER 16	154
CHAPTER 17	164
CHAPTER 18	173
CHAPTER 19	183
CHAPTER 20	193
CHAPTER 21	204

CHAPTER 22	213
CHAPTER 23	224
CHAPTER 24	234
CHAPTER 25	245
CHAPTER 26	254
CHAPTER 27	266
EPILOGUE	277
Connect with Sawyer online	286
About the Author	287

Foreword

So, I have a toddler.

A little girl.

And we read every night.

It's my greatest hope that she inherits my love of reading. She doesn't quite understand what Mommy does for a living, but she knows I write books. She's pulled some from my shelf to look at my picture in the back.

Now, if you've read me widely, you know I write in a variety of sub-genres when it comes to romance. I've done new adult, rom-com, sports romance, straight-up contemporary romance, sweet romance, and, of course, I've done erotic romance.

If you've ready any of my Wicked Horse series, then you know this is my erotic series. You'll also know that this series is not "erotica" as it sometimes gets referred to. The Wicked Horse books are romances with erotic sex scenes.

Why am I even mentioning this?

Because I do worry about how women who write this type of novel are perceived, and I worry about the perception of the women who read these works. Despite the many steps forward we've taken for women to be treated equally, it is somehow deemed wrong by the public for us to even consider reading *gasp* books with sex in them. Forget about it if they have erotic scenes.

I hate this for my daughter. Of course, she's not allowed to read these types of books until she's of age, but I don't want her to be ashamed Mommy writes it, and when she's an adult, I don't want her to be ashamed to read it.

Sex is natural.

Sex is fun.

Sex can be thrilling, adventurous, and even scary sometimes when limits are pushed. The Wicked Horse books will make your eyebrows rise at times. You'll probably blush and sometimes think, "Oh, people really do that type of thing?"

Why, yes, they do.

If you're wondering if I'm writing from personal experience, I have to tell you I'm more well-read and researched than a practical-application kind of gal. Still, I find writing these books to be fun and liberating. They are a way to escape to another world, because that is the point of fiction.

But the books in my Wicked Horse series are about more than sex.

Far more than sex.

There are complex characters you will love and hate. Plots with twists you didn't see coming. Scenes that may have you laughing, and yes… some that will have you sobbing. Those are all the moments you'll remember most about these books (but you will enjoy the sex scenes, too). This is why my books are not erotica. They are not designed for titillation to be the sole purpose. If that happens, so be it, but these are realistic love stories with realistic people, and as such, they are true romances.

Bottom line… I hope you enjoy, and I hope you can do so in an open environment where you don't have to be ashamed to enjoy sexy stories. In fact, feel free to open my book on your Kindle as you sit right next to someone on a plane, a train, or in the hair salon, and be proud that you enjoy reading these works.

I know I sure as hell enjoy bringing them to you.

Love,
Sawyer

CHAPTER 1

Walsh

"WALSH... BUDDY, GOOD to see you," Jerico Jameson says as I saunter into the Social Room of The Wicked Horse.

We shake hands with a strong familiarity born from sharing a woman in bed or a good scotch at the end of an evening. Of course, that was all PT, or pre-Trista. Since then, his cock only fucks his woman, but he's comfortable enough in his relationship that he'll fuck Trista at the Wicked Horse sometimes.

Not going to lie... I enjoy watching.

"Anything special going on tonight?" I ask as I survey the crowd. I always come in late, usually no earlier than eleven. If I wait any longer than that, though, everyone's pretty much worn themselves out for the type of fucking I like.

The deviant, dirty, and often hard kind.

"Same old." Jerico grins as he rattles the ice cubes in his glass as he casually leans against the bar. Unless

Trista's here with him, he usually doesn't venture from either the Social Room or his office.

"I'll make something good then." With a laugh, I lift my chin to the bartender hovering nearby. He nods and turns to get me a bottled water. I don't drink alcohol in here.

Ever.

Not because of any unpleasant experience, not because I don't like the taste, and not because I'm against paying fifteen dollars for two fingers of house brand. Merely because I like feeling the things I do here with all of my senses.

Alcohol loosens inhibitions. However, if my inhibitions were any looser, I'd be having kinky sex in the middle of Las Vegas Boulevard in broad daylight. I like sex, and I don't need to rely on anything to get me in the mood.

But alcohol can also cut down on the feelings. Dull the nerves in my cock, slow my heart rate, and muddle my brain. If I'm going to belong to a sex club, I sure as shit don't want to lose any of those functions.

"How's business?" Jerico asks as I wait for my water.

"It's Vegas and I own a thriving casino," I say with a dry grin. "How do you think it's going?"

Jerico chuckles and nods in understanding, but then says, "I don't get it. You're one of the hottest bachelors in this town, so wealthy most think you've sold your soul to the devil, but then you're here almost every night banging some anonymous chick. You're at an age where you should be getting married and having babies."

I just shake my head and smirk. We've become pretty good friends over the last few years since this club opened, so he should know that's a ludicrous statement to make about me. "Dude… just because you've found the perfect woman and want to spend all your little swimmers in the hopes of making babies doesn't mean every man feels that way."

"Aren't you worried about being alone when you're old and decrepit?" Jerico jokes. "You're what… thirty-five or so?"

"Thirty-six." I take the bottled water from the bartender and push a twenty his way, telling him, "Keep the change."

"Thanks, Walsh," the bartender says. No clue what his name is, but everyone knows my name here. Not only do I put on a good show for the other patrons to enjoy, but I also tip insanely well.

Turning back to Jerico, I feel the need to defend my age and single status. "Besides… did the marriage routine once. Wasn't all that great. And thirty-six is far from being on the verge of going into a nursing home."

"I hear ya, man," Jerico says, and then looks at his watch. "I have to get going. I happen to have a hot-as-hell woman at home waiting for me."

"Have fun," I say with a wink, then turn to walk toward the door that will lead me into a world of debauchery. I told Jerico to have fun, but honestly... fucking his honey on the bed missionary style is not my idea of fun. But more power to him.

As I weave my way through the crowd, I'm stopped a few times by people wanting to chat. Some are men who want to be like me, and so they act like foolish puppies in their hero worship. Some are women wanting a taste of what I can offer.

As many people who stop me, twice as many look away, not wanting to make eye contact. The men who do that are jealous because I get the pick of the women. The women who do it are terrified I might draw them in, and I'm a demanding son of a bitch when I decide to give you my cock. If a woman says "yes" to me, then she'd better be prepared for a wild and bumpy ride that could leave her sore and maybe even a bit bruised.

I'm not every woman's cup of tea.

When I make it to the foyer on the other side of the Social Room, I hesitate for only a minute. I spent last night in the Silo, and I'll be there tomorrow evening for the Masquerade opener. I'm not feeling the Orgy Room right now because I'm also feeling a bit selfish, and in that room, I tend to share the spoils.

Nope. Tonight, I want a more laid-back atmosphere and I want a woman riding me, so I choose The Waterfall Room and turn left.

When I enter, I don't bother to appreciate the lavish decor of high-quality furniture and custom fabrics. I only take a moment to observe the woman lying on her back under the waterfall while some dude eats her out and the water cascades down on them.

After a quick survey, I hone in on an empty couch beside the pool. I uncap my water as I stride there, not making eye contact with anyone. Once I take a swallow, I close the bottle and then set it on the table beside the couch. I undo my belt and pull it free, then unzip my jeans and pull my cock out.

I keep one booted foot firmly on the floor and plant my other on the cushion as I lean back and start to stroke myself.

It takes thirty seconds for a woman to approach me, and I lazily slide my eyes up to take her in. Blonde bombshell.

Enough said.

"Want a ride?" I ask, nodding toward my impressively large erection.

She licks her lips and nods.

"Get naked, then."

She does.

When she starts toward the couch to presumably straddle me, I shake my head. "Get yourself wet for me."

"But I am," she coos.

I reach out with my free hand, push it between legs that spread wide for me, and brush my finger through her bare lips. "Nice piercing," I comment as I brush against warmed metal. She's got a stud above her clit.

When I slip inside, she is indeed wet.

"Feels good," she moans.

I pull my finger free and flick it against her piercing. Her hips buck.

"Condom's in my back pocket." I continue to stroke myself.

The blonde bends over, fantastically huge tits swaying with the motion right in front of my face, and my mouth waters slightly. I'm a total breast man, but, like I said... tonight, I'm feeling selfish.

When she has the condom free of the wrapper, she doesn't need any encouragement from me to put it on. I release my hold on my dick and concentrate on the sensation of her rolling it on.

Making a slight adjustment on the couch, I hold my hand out to her and she takes it. When she has her knees planted beside my hips, she puts her hands on my shoulders for balance. Her eyes are shining brightly as she leans her face closer to mine.

"Been waiting for you to notice me, Walsh," she says breathlessly.

I don't point out that I didn't notice her because that would just be mean, and I don't get off on being cruel.

"Can't wait to have that hot cunt wrapped around me, baby," I say, not bothering to ask her name because I don't care what it is.

But she takes the compliment and lets me guide my cock to her opening. When the tip is nestled in, I release my hold and lean back.

"Go to town," I encourage.

And she does, sliding down on my shaft so swiftly I see the slight wince on her face as she burns from the stretch. My dick is just plain big.

When she bottoms out on me, she pulls her bottom lip between her teeth, which is a sexy-as-fuck move on any woman, and starts to ride.

I hold still, fighting the urge to grab her hips to fuck her hard from beneath. I love doing that to a woman; getting so much power into my upward thrusts I've almost tossed a woman or two off me before.

But tonight, I'm going to let her do the work, because again… feeling selfish.

And she's good, too. Her toned thighs tell me she's an excellent top rider, and she grinds her pussy down hard each time. I want desperately to play around with that stud above her clit, but I'd rather her get off on my cock alone.

I can tell this is a woman who knows how to get it from cock alone, so I let her ride me hard.

I concentrate on those tits bouncing, her little yips of pleasure, and sometimes moans of pain as I swell even bigger inside her.

When she starts to come, she loses some momentum, so my hands come to her hips and I put a little effort into the game.

I punch my hips up, squeezing my ass muscles hard

at the apex, and let gravity pull me back out. In and out, up and down, driving into hot, wet pussy that's got my balls starting to pull inward.

One last powerful drive upward, and I clamp my teeth down and groan out my release. God, it's fucking good.

Never had a bad orgasm in my life, but this one is particularly good.

The woman collapses on top of me, her fingers sifting through my dark shoulder-length hair. I let her lay like that for a moment until I feel myself start to soften, then I'm gently pushing her up and off.

She sits on her haunches, a satisfied smirk on her face like she's the only one who has rocked my world that way. I don't disabuse her of that notion, though.

"Want me to lick you clean?" she asks with a sexy purr, her hands pulling the condom off me.

"No thanks, baby." I gently pick her up and stand her on the floor. Pushing off the couch, I tuck myself into my pants. I pick up my belt and quickly put it back on.

Reaching over, I grab my water bottle before planting a quick kiss on her cheek. "But you were amazing."

I turn around and leave the Waterfall Room.

I don't look back.

CHAPTER 2

Jorie

I SUCK DOWN the last of my wine and put my glass on the bar. "Okay, let's do this."

"Are you sure?" Elena asks.

"Absofuckinglutely," I reply, shoring up my resolve. "But you can't watch me. That would just be too weird."

"You can watch me," she says with a grin.

"Even weirder," I quip and loop my arm through hers.

I let my best friend, Elena, talk me into spending five hundred dollars of money I have no right to spend on a sex club. But the money has been paid, I've had a few glasses of wine, and I need to prove to myself that I am adventurous when it comes to sex.

You see... when your husband wants to separate because you're a "little dull in bed," it makes you want to do really bad things.

I'd moved back home to Henderson, Nevada from Los Angeles three weeks ago after Vince told me to leave our marital home. I'd like to say it was a complete shock, but it wasn't. Things hadn't been right between us for over a year. There was the fighting, which could get vicious because Vince doesn't sugarcoat anything, and there were the hectic work schedules that exhausted me to the point I just wanted to drop into bed at the end of a twelve-hour workday. And yes, there was the fact it was just easier to lay on my back and let him bust a nut so I could just go to sleep, but I didn't think those were things that would unilaterally lead him to call it quits.

There was no discussion.

Just a resounding "no" to my offer to go to counseling.

Hell, I even offered to go to sex therapy with him, but he said he needed space to figure things out.

God, I was confused, and pissed, and depressed, and when it became apparent he really wanted me to leave, it hit hard that my marriage was over.

Elena, my best friend since childhood, was there for me with open arms. Her apartment door was open as well when I arrived with my tail tucked between my legs, a small U-Haul full of boxes that represented almost eight years of married life, and three suitcases. Elena was thrusting a set of keys in my hand before I even crossed the threshold, telling me we were going to be best roommates forever and ever.

I had no family left in Henderson. My mom died during childbirth and my dad when I was seventeen, which meant my older brother Micah got custody of me for a little less than a year before I came of age. I left home at eighteen to go to college in Los Angeles, met and married Vince there, and made a home in sunny California.

It was a little weird coming back to Nevada. Micah lived in San Francisco, and sure… I could have gone there to crash with him and he would have loved it. But I needed a woman to talk to. Someone like Elena who I could shamefully admit to that my husband just didn't find me sexy or thrilling in bed, and that's why he kicked me out.

No way could I ever tell Micah that.

For the past three weeks, Elena has let me live with her rent and obligation free of doing anything other than moping around. I told her all the dirty details of my fall from marital grace, and she assured me Vince was the one fucked in the head, not me.

I didn't believe her, so Elena had a more novel idea to get my head out of my ass.

She suggested I come with her to a sex club she visited on occasion called The Wicked Horse. I was originally horrified at the idea of having casual sex with a complete stranger, but I was also strangely turned on at the same time. That told me that at twenty-eight, my ovaries weren't dried up the way Vince implied they were. In fact, as I mulled over her proposition for a few days, I may have overheated my vibrator with fantasies of what it would be like.

Elena told me all about The Wicked Horse and its various rooms where people could have guilt-free sex in an accepting environment. She explained that vanilla or kinky, one on one, or one on five were only a few options. I could be paddled or gang-banged if I wanted.

From her description, it was my fantasy waiting to happen, and eventually, I just said what the hell and decided to do it, although I was pretty sure it would only be vanilla for me.

Oh, and it helped that tonight is a masquerade event. Not only is it causal sex with a stranger, it's also absolutely anonymous.

It was beyond fun getting ready. Elena and I picked out slutty dresses to wear, mine being nothing more than an electric blue tube dress shot through with silver thread that hugged every inch of my petite five-foot-three frame. Elena chose a slinky gold dress with spaghetti straps and a plunging neckline.

Best of all were our masks. Elena is a hair dresser, but she's also insanely crafty in all things. Instead of a ready-made mask, Elena glued an elaborate design of sapphire blue feathers to my face, interlacing the ends of peacock feathers at my temples. She put my bobbed hair under a tight cap, and then glued feathers all over it as well. My green eyes, which I'd done heavy with smoky shadow, my nose, and my lips were all that were visible. The feathers even caressed my jaw and brushed down along the sides of my neck. It was exquisite, and I wanted to wear them forever and ever. I'd gotten several looks from both men and women, and I felt sexy, mysterious, and beautiful.

And I was going to get laid tonight and prove to myself—and that asshole Vince—that I had it going on in between my legs.

Elena leads me through the main room through a set of double doors and into a foyer with several hallways that lead to the various sex rooms. While I admire Elena and her open sexual nature, I make her promise me again.

"When I decide on someone, you're going to leave the room, right?"

"I promise, Jorie," she says with a squeeze to my arm. "I know it's going to be awkward enough; you don't need your best friend watching."

I stop and turn to face her. "Thank you. You know you're the best thing to ever happen to me, right?"

"Right," she says with a sharp nod. "Now let's go dust the cobwebs off your hoo-hah."

Laughing, she turns me to the right and we head down the hall that says The Silo.

This was my preference as she told me there were a few rooms in The Silo that had curtains that could be drawn in case I got a little shy and didn't want people watching. I have no clue what my preference will be because I'm half expecting to bolt out of here the minute

I get my first look at the debauchery.

When we walk in, my breath is sucked from my lungs as I look around.

People having sex everywhere.

On couches, on the floor. Standing up against the wall.

And then my eyes take in the glass-walled rooms on the perimeter of the circular Silo, and I suck in a hard breath. There's a room with a set of stocks. A woman is locked inside while a guy fucks her mouth gently, and another has his face buried in her ass.

Another room has a man tied to a St. Andrew's cross, getting his dick sucked by a man and a woman taking turns on him.

And still another room where there's a mattress with a single couple getting their sixty-nine on.

"Hot, right?" Elena breathes into my ear. A shiver runs up my spine as my panties get drenched with a rush of moisture.

"Oh, wow," I tell her softly. "I never could have imagined this."

"See anything you like?" she asks me slyly.

And yes, I see a lot I like. I look around at the people, immediately noting several men staring at me and Elena hungrily behind their masks.

I'm so getting laid tonight.

And then, I see *him*.

Him.

A fucking god.

Wearing nothing but a pair of faded jeans that hang low on lean hips, above which rises a trail of dark hair that stops at his navel. He's not the type of guy who struts around flexing his abs, but I could tell if he did, they'd be washboard perfection. Muscular chest and arms, but in a toned way.

Tanned skin.

No, not tanned… olive.

Exotic.

And that's all I can see because he's hooded. His entire head is covered in a form-fitting leather mask. It must be laced or zipped up the back, revealing only a pair of golden-brown eyes, full lips, and dark, longish hair.

"God, he's magnificent," Elena whispers as he walks from the opposite side of the room.

No, not walks.

He prowls, but not toward any particular prey. Arms hanging loose but swinging slightly in that confident way that says, "I'm the fucking shit and I know it." The confidence exuding from him is sexy as hell.

He doesn't look at anyone, just quickly walks down a short hall in between two of the rooms and disappears.

I'm slightly dizzy because I've forgotten to breathe, and I take in a shaky lungful of air. When I let it out slowly, I register abject disappointment that he's gone.

"Oh, this is interesting," Elena murmurs as she

nudges me in the shoulder. I follow her gaze to one of the previously unoccupied rooms. It's now lit up.

The masked man is in there. He's all alone except for some type of furniture that's covered completely in a silk sheet. Casually walking up to it, he takes the material in hand. He pulls it off not with a magician's flourish, but slowly so the object is revealed.

And it's a…

Well, I'm not quite sure what it is. He walks around it, blocking it from my view for a moment. People move toward the glass to get a better look. Before I know it, my legs are moving, too, and Elena follows me so we are standing right in front of the room, the sexy, mysterious man no more than five feet from us on the other side.

He is doing something with the contraption, and when he finally moves away to face the crowd, I vaguely register people gasping.

But my eyes are pinned on him as his gaze sweeps the crowd.

"Holy shit," Elena mutters. "That is some freaky shit."

My body jolts at the heat in her words, and I follow her gaze. My pussy floods with wetness at the sight.

At first glance, it looks like one of those portable massage chairs where a person straddles the seat and leans forward to put their face in a cut-out cushioned headrest. But there is no headrest, just an inclined padded bench that extends forty-five degrees away from the seat that's meant to be straddled.

The seat, if it can be called that, is square, padded, and covered with leather, with a square opening in the center.

"What is it?" I ask.

"No clue," she says, but then it becomes clear to everyone as the man reaches into a compartment attached to the side of the unit and pulls out a flesh-colored dildo that must be eight inches. It is so life-like I can see a thick vein running up the side.

He bends over, and my jaw drops as he hooks it onto a contraption under the seat, causing about four inches to poke up through the center.

There is no doubt in anyone's mind now that seat is meant to be straddled by a woman with the dildo inside of her.

All I can think is, *Who came up with this idea?*

Next thing is, *I wonder what that would feel like?*

The man straightens. Still not looking at anyone, he fishes inside his front pocket where he pulls out a tube of lipstick.

He walks up to the glass window and starts writing words in reverse fashion so we can read them from our side of the glass.

Slowly, he spells out his message.

Anyone brave enough to come in here with me?

"I'm going unless you call dibs," Elena says to me quickly, her eyes pinned on the man.

"Dibs," I hurry to say, even though my blood pressure spikes when I realize I just committed myself.

She turns to look at me with a bright smile. "That's my girl."

About five women now push their way up to the glass, one of them literally knocking me to the side. I wobble briefly on my heels as the women raise their hands and start calling through the glass, "Me. Me. Me."

My heart sinks as I realize that while I might be walking toward an adventurous orgasm, I'm going to have to compete to get there, and that is something I just don't have within me. I've always been more of the wallflower and never the aggressor, and I can't handle the rejection. Not after getting rejected by Vince.

I start to turn away when a loud knocking on the glass startles me into looking back.

The masked man is staring at me, his index finger pointed in my direction. He nods, turns his hand, and then crooks his finger, beckoning me in there.

I'm immediately filled with doubt and fear, and Elena must sense it for she calls out loud enough the guy has to hear, "She'll be right there."

He nods and turns away, then Elena has my hand as she drags me down the short hall.

"I can't," I practically screech.

"You can," she growls. "You called dibs… and there's no going back on dibs."

Before I know it, she's led me down the hall to the

rear perimeter of the glass rooms. She opens the door, pushing me in so hard I stumble.

As she slams the door, she calls out, "I'm leaving. Find me in the Social Room when you're done. If you can walk that is."

With my heart beating so hard I'm afraid I'm going to die, I turn slowly around to find the man looking at me. He's so much larger being in the same room with him, and my fear spikes higher.

"Panties off," he says. "Leave the rest on."

I stare at him, frozen.

"Panties off or leave," he says, not in a mean or condescending way, but just in a matter-of-fact one.

When I look back on this moment, I know it will be a defining one for me. I think of Vince telling me that I just didn't do it for him anymore. After a glance at the man who is already hard beneath the denim of his jeans, I make my decision.

I pull my dress up just high enough to grab my panties, and I shimmy them down my legs, kicking them free.

"Good girl," he praises and holds out a hand.

My legs tremble as they move forward, but I place my palm against his. When his fingers curl around mine, engulfing me so completely, I feel an electrical spark of desire join the blood racing through my veins.

Without a word, he leads me to the contraption. I falter when I look outside the glass, horrified at the crowd gathered. Women glaring at me. Men looking like they want to devour me.

"The curtains," I practically whimper. "Close them."

He doesn't answer, only pulls me right to the seat and growls his order. "Straddle it."

My eyes shoot to his, and I see no patience within the warm brown depths. He's so stern and intimidating, yet his eyes are glowing with a clear promise that this will be good.

Within them, I also see that the curtains are going to stay open, and I think I may have made a mistake.

"I won't hurt you," he says in a soothing voice.

"Promise?" I whisper.

"Straddle it," he says again, this time with a gentle coaxing filled with promise.

"Oh, God," I moan, but then I lift a leg to straddle the seat.

CHAPTER 3

Walsh

MY ENTIRE FUCKING body is vibrating with need, and this is a cause for concern as I haven't felt this way in forever. My life is filled with luxury—penthouse apartment, fast cars, the best champagne, and let's not forget the never-ending supply of sex I get at The Wicked Horse.

When I walk in this place, I'm always filled with lust.

I always leave satisfied.

But I can't remember a time I've gotten hard just by seeing a woman. I can't remember a time that I've seen a woman and needed her more than anything I've ever needed before.

Sounds dramatic, but fuck if I can explain the way I almost had a heart attack when this woman in sapphire and peacock feathers started to walk away from the glass. She was interested and turned on when she saw my little contraption, but it was obvious she wasn't going to fight for the right to straddle it.

I must remember to find her friend later and figure out a way to thank her properly for practically dragging this feathered beauty into my room. I'm playing hardball with her, taking a gamble that by taking away her control, it will make her want to stay, but there's no way I'm letting her walk out that door.

The contraption is special. I should have named it with an honorary title as it was custom made and brought in for tonight's event with Jerico's permission. So many things can be done with it, but only one I want to do right now.

It's set up about five feet from the glass and parallel to it. The minute she lifts her leg over the seat, I walk around to stand behind her.

She's trembling—from fear, excitement, or both, I don't know—but I move in close and bring my hands to her hips. She's tiny and I tower over her, something that causes my dick to get harder since I could easily break her if I wanted.

Leaning down, I place my lips near an ear that has the tip of a peacock feather just barely covering it and murmur in a deep voice, "Why did you come in here?"

She shakes her head, not in denial of giving me an answer but because I don't think she has the power to speak. Her legs are spread over the seat but locked tight, and it's going to take some coaxing to get her to do what I want. The dildo isn't dainty, and it's going to take some maneuvering to get it inside what I'm betting is the sweetest and wettest pussy in the club tonight. I can just sense it. I could put my hand between her legs and find out, but I don't need to.

"Relax," I growl, not even recognizing my own voice. It's thick with lust, need, and a darkness I've never heard before.

I tilt my head to run my lips down her neck.

She shudders, and I smile.

Perfect.

"Bend your knees," I order.

She does nothing for a moment, but to my surprise, she complies and starts to squat lower over the seat. Her whimper about slays me.

Without taking my hands from her hips, I lean my body to the left and watch her descend. Closer and closer to the head of the dildo, the stretchy material of her dress riding up higher on her pale thighs.

When she makes contact, her head falls back and full, cherry-painted lips part with a gasp.

"That's it." My voice is more guttural, almost otherworldly, and it's an indication of how turned on I am. "Rotate your hips, Feather."

"Not my name," she whispers. It surprises me she has the cognizance to formulate words at this point. I can feel how lost she is to the moment.

"It is tonight," I tell her. "Now, move those hips. Work it in."

And fuck... she does. Slow, circular movements as

she pushes down on the dildo. Her breath coming in sharp little pants of need. I can feel my cock leaking, wetting the denim of my jeans. My fingers dig into her hips, helping to push her down.

"Feels… good," she gasps as she rocks her way onto the thick latex.

Twisting my head, I turn to look out the glass and I can feel the hardcore lust coming off the people watching. This is what I really get off on… the exhibitionism… but when I see a man standing there with his dick out of his pants, stroking it hard as he watches my feathered bird, I have an insane moment where I want to close the curtains to block out the world.

"It's in," she moans as her ass hits the seat, and what a picture she makes as I turn to examine her.

Legs spread wide, just the tips of her toes pressed into the concrete floor. Her hands are on her thighs, her nails digging into her own creamy skin.

Yeah… not all the way in, but I'm going to rectify that.

"Hold still." I bend to take her wrists, pulling her arms up to the inclining bench in front of her and pushing her hands to the padding. Without my command, she grips the leather covering at the edges, her knuckles going white. I glance down and see her eyes closed tight, lips pressed into a hard line.

"Going to make an adjustment," I tell her so she's not taken by surprise. "Lean forward a bit."

She does with a tiny moan as the flexibility of the dildo causes it to move within her. Squatting down behind her, I reach under the contraption and pull on a lever with one hand while my other holds the padded seat. I push it up, angling it toward the inclined bench. It pushes her body forward, and she cries out in surprise as her chest is pushed into the incline. The reverse angle of the seat to the padded incline, along with half the dildo wedged in her pussy, has her pinned in place.

Just fucking perfect.

"This is going to get intense," I tell her quietly. "Just hold on and don't move."

"Okay," she murmurs, her voice tight with anticipation.

God, I hope she holds on and doesn't jump off once I fire this baby up.

Reaching under the bench, I flip an electric switch. The engine gives a faint purr as the dildo—which is attached to a jackhammer-type stud—starts to move slowly inside of her.

"Fuck," she screams as it pulls out and gives her the four inches plus another two, but she doesn't move.

"Easy." I put a hand on her lower back. "Let it do the work."

"Oh, God. Oh, God. Oh, God."

With my fingertips, I pull the skirt up to bare her ass, almost coming as I watch the dildo working in and out of her from behind.

"Christ," I mutter as I stare mesmerized for a moment.

"So good," she moans as she turns her face to lay her feathered cheek on the padded bench, away from the glass window. She opens her eyes, and her stare is blissed out and blank.

Standing straight, I take a few faltering steps back, my hand involuntarily going to my cock to rub it through my jeans. I do this briefly before reaching into my front pocket, pushing past the tube of lipstick I'd put back in there after writing my invitation on the glass, and pulling out the tiny remote control.

I hesitate for only a moment before I push an upward arrow button to increase the speed. The other button, I leave alone because it would increase the depth. She's so tiny, and I don't want to hurt her. I'll leave it at six inches.

The dildo-vibrator now hammers faster into her pussy. Shiny wet pussy juices shimmer on it, but my gaze slides to her face. A single tear of desperation falls out of her eye and soaks the feather below it. I hit the speed button one more notch, and she starts to moan.

Jesus… this is better than I ever thought could happen with this machine, and I have to let Micah see the fruits of his labor.

I jam my hand into my back pocket, tag my phone and pull it out. I don't hesitate in the slightest pulling up the camera. The woman is unidentifiable with her body still mostly covered, no identifying tattoos or marks I could see, and her face and head covered with feathers. She's simply my bird right now, but Micah has got to see this baby in action.

He's the one that built it for me, after all. A true engineering marvel.

My fingers shake as I take a picture of the entire contraption fucking the woman, then I zoom in and take a close up of the dildo stroking her pussy.

I fire them off to Micah followed by a quick text message. *You are fucking brilliant.*

I don't expect him to reply, but his responding "ding" causes me to look at my phone. *Goddamn. I've got a hard-on.*

Ditto, I respond. *But I'm going to get mine taken care of very soon.*

Asshole, he replies. *Call me later and give me details*.

Oh, I totally will. He's going to want not just the details about how hard this makes her come, but he's also going to want to know how well the machine works. It's not the first he's built, but it's the best. His goal of starting a high-end, custom-built sex machine business looks like it might be more than just an idea over beers now. While his real job as a mechanical engineer pays him well, he's got a kinky side he likes to explore.

I shove my phone back in my pocket and walk up to the woman getting fucked by a jack-hammering dildo. Moving around to the side of the machine so I can see her face, I squat so we are eye to eye. Her focus is gone, completely glazed over. She's making tiny little whimpers.

Looking down to the remote, I hit the depth button and give her another inch.

The corresponding groan causes my balls to start to ache.

"Going to come, Feather?" I ask.

She tries to focus on me, but there's no coming back from the deep sexual subspace she's in. I watch her face carefully as more tears seep into the feathers, darkening the sapphire blue to cobalt. I reach a hand out, caress her jaw lightly.

And then I'm absolutely mesmerized as she starts to orgasm. I expected it to take her hard, but it rolls through her rather slowly. It ripples from her spine to her shoulders where she starts a full-body shudder.

Her eyes squeeze shut, more tears spill, and she lets out a long, low moan that goes on and on and on.

My finger hits the red stop button on the remote. While the dildo powers down slowly, I'm pulling a condom out and ripping it open. Doing nothing more than pushing my jeans past my hips, I spring my cock free and cover it up.

Lust pulses through me so hard I'm practically dizzy with the need to fuck her. She starts to regain some conscious focus and manages an, "Oh, fuck," as I release the lever on the seat and pull her off with a wet sucking sound.

Turning to the glass, I pick her up, wrap her legs around my waist, and drive into her using her back against the glassed wall for leverage.

She screams and I almost come, so I just hold still as I bend my face to bite at her bare shoulder. "So sexy," I praise.

Then I fuck her.

Up against the glass as the crowd watches, getting a great look at my cock stretching her already-overused pussy from behind.

"Fuck, fuck, fuck," I mutter, surprising myself. I normally don't let my words get in the way.

She in turn moans, "More, more, more."

"Greedy little bird," I growl as I hurl my body into hers, as deep as I've ever been in a woman.

She tightens all around me, a quick hard orgasm causing her to scream as her head falls back and hits the glass. I look down, seeing her beautiful tits jiggling under the material of her blue dress.

I bring a hand up, test the weight of one breast, and squeeze it lightly. Her head flies up, and she looks down at me. I bring my eyes up to hers, and we lock. Those eyes are magnificent… bright. Almost lime in color.

I pinch her nipple through the material, and her eyes harden with need. Snaking my fingers up, I pull the material down over the left breast and pop it free. She rotates her hips and grinds down on me, a silent plea for more. I take her nipple in between my thumb and forefinger and rotate it hard.

She bucks against me, and my balls shrink tight. I grab the material again, in the middle, and drag it down so I can see more of her gorgeous tits, the other one springing free with the nipple already begging me to torture it. I flick it with my middle finger and fuck me standing… she starts to orgasm again.

It's all over for me. I slam into her repeatedly, my cock swelling and then exploding viciously as I watch her breasts jiggle from the pounding.

And that's when I see it.

A crescent-shaped scar on the side of her right breast, raised and puffy.

What the fuck?

My eyes travel further down, and there's a corresponding scar on the side of her breast that looks almost identical except it's a bit smaller.

Oh, Jesus fuck, no.

The sight of those scars repulses me as much as they excite me… because I realize who I have in my arms. Whose pussy I'm claiming right now, and Christ… another violent ripple of pleasure courses through me with a secondary orgasm, but I've got nothing left in my balls to unload.

My eyes snap up to hers as my hips still move so I can prolong the best damn pleasure of my life.

Fucking goddamn Jorie Pearce.

Micah's little sister.

CHAPTER 4

Jorie

I CAN TELL the moment something changes between me and this man who just ruined me for life. After giving me the best sex of my entire life… after freeing me from myself… he turns inward and closes off.

I know he came. Maybe even twice.

But his eyes right now are blazing with fury, and I don't want to see it.

I don't want to know what I did wrong, or how bad I was, so I close my eyes against it.

His hand comes to my jaw, gripping it hard enough to get my attention. My eyelids spring open. It's not lost on me that he's still moving slowly within me, yet he looks at me like I'm repulsive.

"Let me down," I mutter as my hands push against his chest.

He complies immediately, pulling out of me and setting me down so fast my legs buckle and I fall to my knees. Taking two steps back from me, he pulls the condom off and tosses it near a garbage can against the adjacent wall. It falls short and hits the concrete as I push back up.

"Cover yourself up," he snaps as he tucks himself back into his jeans, zipping them up.

I pull my dress down over my bare ass, feeling wetness between my legs that's evidence of my own arousal and not his semen. It shames me greatly, and then I'm quickly covering my breasts with the material.

Before I know what's happening, he's got his huge hand clamped around my upper arm and pulling me to the door. He pauses just long enough to bend over and swipe my panties off the ground, shoving them in his front pocket.

I struggle to keep up with his long legs, which is difficult given the four-inch heels Elena talked me into wearing. My legs are weak, and I'm so confused over the fact I can feel little tremors of pleasure still pulsing between my legs.

It's in vain when I try to jerk my arm free, and fear fills me when he drags me out of the glassed room, out of The Silo, down another hall that says Private, and into a locker room I suspect is for employees.

"Goddamn it, Jorie," the man says as he turns me to face him while still gripping me tightly.

"Ow, you asshole," I grit out as I successfully jerk my arm away from him and rub it. "What the hell?"

He just stares at me with hard, flat eyes.

"Wait," I say as a shiver runs up my spine that has nothing to do with a residual orgasm and everything to do with apprehension. "Did you just call me Jorie?"

His shoulders drop almost in defeat and his head sags so he's looking at the floor. Almost wearily, he loosens a tie at the back and pulls the mask over his head. When he looks back at me, my legs go numb.

I stumble back two feet, my ass coming up hard against a locker that rattles. "No."

Walsh Brooks stares at me without an ounce of contrition for what he just did to me, but he's clearly distressed if the darkness in his eyes is any indication.

"What in the fuck are you doing here?" he growls, and his voice is different from what I'd heard in that glass room. It hits me all at once that the voice I'd heard in there was Walsh Brooks amped up on kink and lust, which was why his words came out all gravely and loaded with desire, changing it so much I hadn't heard anything that resembled the man I knew.

I haven't seen him in almost ten years, and so much has changed about him. Gone is the shaven, clean-cut executive. Before me stands a man who looks like a rock god. But he's not that either. He's very much a businessman who owns a casino here in Vegas. He's a millionaire probably a million times over.

But his hair is just down to his shoulders, dark as sin and slightly wavy as it falls back from a middle part. His fawn-brown eyes are the same, straight nose and cut cheekbones, but he's wearing a trimmed beard that runs just along his jawline and it's so damn sexy.

Then again… Walsh was always the sexiest man I'd ever seen regardless of how he wore his hair. I'd crushed on him hard in my teens, and even after I turned eighteen and headed to Los Angeles, I tended to compare men I'd dated and slept with to him.

Except when I married Vince. When I did that, Vince was it for me, and I didn't think about Walsh in any fashion other than being a family friend.

A dear, devoted friend with whom I have no business doing what I just did.

I just stare into his hard eyes, trying to reconcile that I just had sex with Walsh Brooks, best friend to my brother Micah, and my onetime hero when I needed one the most.

No, not just sex. Fabulous, dirty, kinky, unrestrained, mind-blowing—

"Answer me, damn it."

I jump in fright over the edge in his voice. "I don't know," I say lamely.

This seems to piss Walsh off as in two strides, he's hulking over me, his bulky frame so intimidating I find myself shrinking away from him.

"Don't act scared of me, Jorie," he snaps as he places his palms on the locker beside my head. "I was just balls deep inside of you, and you've known me your entire life. But I want to know… why the fuck was I just balls deep inside of you?"

I'm going to hell. The vivid reminder of what we just did causes a surge of wetness between my legs. It's not quite a moan that escapes my mouth, but it must sound like it because I swear flames leap in Walsh's eyes.

"You want it again, don't you?" he murmurs as he studies me closely.

I shake my head in a bald-faced lie.

"Micah's baby sister, all grown up, and I'm betting drenched for it again," he mutters.

Shit… I can feel something warm running down the inside of my leg, so I press them together.

"You're squirming, Jorie," he taunts.

"I'm not," I lie again.

Walsh is pissed this happened, but that anger is waning. Instead, the more he talks, the more his eyes become heated. His voice is sensual, not condemning.

"Will it help if I admit that I want you again?" he asks, but rather than wait for my answer, he's dragging my hand to his crotch where I feel his hard thickness pressing against his jeans.

I swallow hard, and even though I should pull my hand away, I curl my fingers around him and squeeze. Walsh's eyes flutter closed and his forehead wrinkles with what appears to be pained distress.

"Except I can't fucking have you because you're Micah's little sister," he snarls as he tears away from me. He paces back and forth, scrubbing his fingers through his long hair to pull it away from his face before letting it go again as he turns to me.

He stares at me thoughtfully for a moment and then asks, "Where's your friend?"

"That was Elena," I say quietly.

"That was Elena?" he asks through gritted teeth. He knows Elena as well since she's been my best friend my entire life.

I nod. "She said she'd meet me in the Social Room."

Walsh nods curtly. "Alright… let's go."

"Where?" I ask as I push off the locker.

"I'll escort you back to her, then you two are getting the hell out of here and never coming back," he mutters as he holds a hand out to me.

I'll admit, I've been more than a bit rattled since Walsh revealed himself to me. But I've taken about all his domineering ways that I can handle for today.

"Go to hell, Walsh." I put my hands on my hips and narrow my eyes. "You aren't my keeper. I don't do what you say."

Wrong words, apparently, because he's on me in a nanosecond, backing me right into the lockers again. "You don't do what I say? You fucking impaled that sweet pussy on a dildo because I told you to, Jorie. You were so hot for it, you would have done anything I told you to."

I know Walsh is only trying to get me out of here, but his words are incredibly shaming to me. He has no clue what it took for me to come here and give into this challenge for myself personally.

For my fucking self-esteem.

"Fuck you," I snarl, pushing past him and starting for the locker room door.

"Jorie, wait," he calls, an apology in his voice. That just pisses me off even more, and I walk faster. My hand hits the handle to swing open the door, but his palm is there, holding it shut. "Just… wait a minute, okay?"

I don't turn to face him, feeling the heat from his body against my back. "Let me out," I murmur.

"Why did you come here?" he asks again, this time almost pleading. "And please tell me I didn't scar you for life with that… that…"

I whip around to face him, and he takes a cautious step back. "With that impaling of my sweet pussy?" I ask with derision.

He ignores my taunt and, to my surprise, lifts his hands to my face. His fingers run along the feathers from my temple across my forehead, and then he finds what he wants. He carefully peels the cap off my head, releasing my hair, which I'm sure looks horrid after being stuck under there. I give it an unconscious shake, and the flat crop of bangs that are cut severely over my forehead falls forward.

"You cut your hair," he says as his eyes roam over me. I had indeed cut my long, almost black hair to just below my jawline in an angular bob. Vince had been all about the long hair, but it clearly wasn't enough to get his dick up, so I had Elena lop it off a few weeks ago.

I lift a nervous hand, tucking the hair back on one side, but I don't respond.

"Why were you here?" he asks for a third time, dropping his hands to his side.

"It's personal," I return, my gaze dropping to the floor.

"Come on, Jorie." He pushes my face back up with his fingers under my chin. "It's me."

"It's you," I agree. "But I don't know you anymore. Haven't seen you for ten years. You didn't even come to my wedding."

A muscle in his jaw starts to tick, but he remains committed to finding the truth. "I take it you're not married anymore?"

"What makes you ask that?"

"Because the Jorie Pearce I know wouldn't step out on her husband," he says simply.

"We're separated," is all I'm willing to give.

"And you're what… here to break the single life back in?"

"Something like that," I mutter.

"Bullshit," he says harshly. "Now quit screwing around and just tell me why I had the hottest, dirtiest sex imaginable with the one person I should have never done that with?"

"Because I don't think I'm any good at it," I yell, then immediately cringe with embarrassment. My voice drops about ten decibels to a mere whisper. "I'm here to find out if that's true or not."

Walsh's head jerks in surprise. "Why would you think that?"

"Vince told me that when he kicked me out of our house," I mutter as I turn my face to the side to stare at the lockers.

"I'll fucking kill that bastard," Walsh growls, and my eyes snap back to him.

His face is awash with fury. I know from very personal experience that Walsh may not kill Vince, but he'd beat him so bad he'd wish he were dead. Walsh has done it before to a man on my behalf.

"It doesn't matter," I say upon a long, tired sigh. I drop my gaze once again, suddenly feeling a million years old and wanting nothing more than to climb into bed.

To my surprise, Walsh steps back from me and gestures toward the door. "You should get going."

My eyes slide up and lock with his for a moment. Then I nod and turn for the door.

"Jorie." My name comes out on a sigh, and I turn to look over my shoulder. "You were magnificent. Best sex of my life."

I give him a small smile. I don't know if that's true or not, but that is the Walsh I know. He would be the one who would do whatever he could to take away my pain.

I also know that from personal experience.

"Thanks," I say before I walk out the door.

CHAPTER 5

Walsh

I POUR MYSELF some vodka and add a few ice cubes to the glass. As I sip at it, I flip through my playlist, choosing some Fiona Apple. She filters through my apartment on Bluetooth speakers.

My mind is all kinds of fucked up over what happened tonight.

I wasn't lying to Jorie. Best sex ever.

Most wrong sex ever.

I don't want to even think about the fact I sent her brother a fucking picture of her.

Picking up my glass, I pad through my living room with its floor-to-ceiling glass walls that look out over Vegas, then into my bedroom. I should take a shower but sick bastard that I am, I don't want to wash the smell of Jorie off me just yet. I've lusted after her for as long as I knew what true lust was, and when that first happened, she was way too young for me to be thinking those things. The differences in our age assured that.

Jorie had been a constant in my life for a very long time, right along with her brother Micah. Even though there's an eight-year age difference between Jorie and me, there's just a two-year gap between Micah and me. We were neighbors and because Jorie's mom died having her, Micah had a lot of babysitting duty as he got older. It was unfair to put that burden on a kid, but Jorie's father, Gregory, was practically absent from their lives.

He was an attorney who had met and married Micah's mom, who was a Vegas showgirl. She left the life to move to the suburbs of Henderson, bringing her five-year-old son with her. Gregory never did really take to Micah even though he adopted him and gave him his last name. He was more interested in the beautiful wife he got in Rhonda Webb, and I'm guessing he adopted her son to make her happy. Micah and I talked about that a lot as we were growing up because he spent most of his time at my house next door. His biological dad had been a one-night stand, so he never knew who he was. Micah's mom died so young that my parents naturally took him under their wing. That was just their way.

I have no clue if Gregory ever really wanted Rhonda to get pregnant, but she did, and Jorie came into this world looking just like her mom and brother. In fairness to Gregory, he may have ignored Micah most of the time, but he doted on Jorie whenever the nanny was off duty.

And Micah never held that against his little sister.

On the contrary, he was and still is very close to her, despite their age difference. Because Micah was often left in charge of Jorie whenever Gregory was too busy to be bothered, I was right there alongside him, helping to watch the little black-haired, green-eyed terror who grew into an immense beauty. She may have been a pain in our asses on most occasions, but I adored her the same as Micah.

Micah and Jorie's bond is tight, made even more so when Jorie's dad died just as she entered her senior year in high school. Micah left his job in Michigan to move back to Henderson as her guardian so she could finish school where all her friends were. After she went off to UCLA, he went on to San Francisco, where he's been ever since.

Setting my glass on the nightstand, I take my clothes off and just let them drop to the floor. I crawl naked into bed, giving a brief glance to my well satisfied dick before I flip the sheet over my lap.

Seeing those goddamn scars on Jorie's breast threw me over hard tonight. I was in mid-orgasm when I saw them, overwhelmed with rage over what had caused those scars, and having my climax fire up for a second time as I realized it was Jorie on my cock.

Talk about a mind fuck, but then again, I'd always wanted her.

She was only fifteen when I first masturbated to dirty thoughts about her. I was fucking twenty-three and jerking off because I'd come home to visit my parents and saw Jorie in the backyard in her bathing suit. She's always been pale—can't tan to save her life—and she was utterly fucking delectable. She'd developed early, and her breasts were practically spilling out of her top. I fucking craved a taste of her… wanted to put my mouth between her legs, and that's what I imagined as I jacked myself off in the shower.

Goddamn perverted is what it was.

Of course, I shut that shit firmly down after what happened to her just a year later when she was sixteen. My stomach churns as I remember her call to me.

"Jorie?" I'd answered hesitantly. She never called me, not because I didn't care about her or vice-versa, but we weren't friends. She was just the little toddler who would chase Micah and me around the yard. She was the middle-school kid who needed help with her science project, and Micah and I did the whole thing for her. And yeah, she was the teenage girl I fantasized about a few times because she was hot as hell and totally off-limits, which made her even hotter for some reason.

I didn't hear anything at first, but then her voice came across so frail. "I need help, Walsh."

She was in a hotel suite not too far from my office. I'd gotten into real-estate development and worked for a major firm in Vegas trying to soak up all the knowledge I could with the goal one day to own my own business. I was working super late, which was par for the course for me.

When I arrived, I noted the suite had been cleared of the thirty-plus high schoolers who had been partying there that night to celebrate the end of their junior year. I found Jorie covered in blood in the bathroom, holding a towel to her breast. The long, twelve-inch piece of glass that had broken from a vase in the shape of a dagger lay on the floor beside her.

It never once occurred to me that Jorie had tried to harm herself. I knew her well enough to know that wasn't what happened.

I didn't think someone tried to stab her, either.

By the torn panties wrapped around one of her ankles and the shattered vase, I got what happened. She'd been attacked and hurt in the struggle.

"Oh, Jesus fuck," I'd groaned when I saw her sitting against the vanity, clutching the bloody towel to her chest. I went down to my knees beside her, shards of glass cutting through my dress pants and into my skin. "What happened, Jorie?"

Her teeth were chattering so badly she couldn't talk at first, but then she managed to say, "There were two of them, but I fought them off. They got scared when they saw the blood and took off."

Relief flooded through me. She'd not been raped, but those white panties around her ankle told me she'd come damn close.

"Let me see," I said as I gently pulled her hands away from the towel. She winced as I did so, and I took in the two

wounds, surmising that when the vase broke, that long piece went through her breast like a damned sword. But it clearly wasn't life threatening as the bleeding seemed to be contained.

I pressed the towel back and assured her, "It's okay. It's going to be okay."

She never cried. Only her teeth chattered as I lifted her up and carried her through the broken glass. I laid her on a couch in the main living area and called an ambulance.

I never left her side. She didn't call Micah because he was working in Michigan at the time for an engineering firm there. Jorie's dad was on a business trip. She was sixteen and perfectly capable of staying by herself for a few days.

Or so everyone thought.

I held her hand while they stitched her up, and I contained my rage when she refused to involve the police. She convinced me to keep my mouth shut, and then explained to the doctor that she slipped in the bathroom, causing a freak accident when the vase shattered and stabbed through her breast.

When we were waiting to get discharged, I pushed her to tell me why she wouldn't report it.

"I was drunk, Walsh," she said softly. "Maybe I was asking for it."

"Don't ever let me hear you talk that way again," I'd chastised her, but there was a hard edge to my voice that made her eyes go round.

"Don't tell Micah or my dad," she pleaded. "They'll be so mad."

I warred with myself over what to do, but by the time I had her in my car to drive the forty-five minutes to Henderson, I agreed not to tell them on one condition.

Though it was with great reluctance, she gave me the names of the boys who tried to take something that didn't belong to them and left her a bloody mess on the bathroom floor.

They bled more than she did when I was done with them, and it was mine and Jorie's secret forever.

I grab my glass, taking a long swallow of the vodka. Pulling my photos up on my phone, I flip to the two I'd snapped of Jorie tonight and grit my teeth to stave off the regret.

Fuck, she's gorgeous.

Guilt overwhelms me as I realize I'm totally turned on by a photo of her sitting on that contraption built by her older brother. Disgust practically curdles my blood as I think about Micah seeing that picture.

Christ, what a mess.

I flip to my texts and see a lengthy line of messages from the man himself.

Dude… I've been waiting for details.

How did it work? Any problems? Any adjustments to the design?

Is there video? Please tell me you took video?

So… did it get her pussy warmed up for you?

I wince. It sure had.

I fucked your little sister, Micah, because I was so turned on by that fucking machine you built and the way she came all over your goddamned dildo, I think to myself.

"Fuck," I yell out to the emptiness of my bedroom and hurl my glass to the side where it crashes against the wall. I let my head fall back against the headboard and close my eyes.

Images of Jorie working herself down onto that latex cock.

Images of Jorie coming on mine.

I open my eyes with a growl, confident I'm never going to be able to sleep again because I can't close my eyes.

The ringing of my phone startles me, and it's a welcomed interruption. When I glance down to see Micah calling, I groan in complete misery over this mess.

Taking a deep breath, I let it out and answer, "It's three in the morning. Don't you ever sleep?"

"Don't you ever answer your texts?" he returns with a laugh, and I can tell he's drunk by the slight slur to his voice. Micah always parties hard and it's a Saturday night, so there's no surprise he's inebriated. "What the fuck, buddy? You send me a picture of a fine ass riding my cock machine and you can't spare more details?"

I wince, thinking he'd straight out slit my throat if he knew who that fine ass belonged to. "It worked like a charm," I tell him, my tongue thickened with the deception that's rolling off.

"Did the remote-control work okay?" he asks, his words still slurred but the question indicating he's not so drunk that he left his engineering degree behind.

"Yeah," I say, then give a cough to clear my throat. "I didn't test the full depth and had it at medium speed. Jerico's going to let some other people test it out and said he'll pass notes on to you."

"How many times did she come?" he asks lecherously.

"Once," I tell him honestly.

"And let me guess… once again on your cock?"

Twice, actually.

"She wasn't all that great," I find myself lying to him so he'll quit asking so many fucking questions.

"Probably because you couldn't jack hammer her the way my machine did." He breaks off into peals of laughter, but I remain quiet.

"Dude… what's wrong with you?" Micah asks because he's my best friend—like my brother—and I never hesitate to share the nitty-gritty details of my sex life if he asks. We've been swapping personal porn stories for years.

"Nothing man," I say in a tired voice, but I'm more fatigued from the stress of tonight than anything.

"Alright," he says, his voice clearly unsure if he accepts what I'm saying. But thankfully, he lets it go. "I'll get up with you in a few days. I'm thinking about taking a trip down there."

"Why?" I ask a little too defensively. "I mean… didn't you just take a week off to go to Cabo last month?"

"Yeah, but I got more vacation time and I want to check on Jorie," he tells me. "Hey… I told you she left Vince, didn't I? I guess things weren't working out between them, and she's back in Henderson. Staying at Elena's."

This is fucking great. I know more about the fall of Jorie's marriage than her brother does. He thinks it was a mutual split, and I happen to know that prick told Jorie she sucked in bed and then kicked her out.

I want to kill him.

"Yeah, I think you mentioned that," I say evasively before wrapping things up. "Listen, man… I'm beat. Going to call it a night, but let me know if you're headed down this way. You can stay with me, of course."

"Of course," he says in agreement. "No way am I crashing at Elena's little apartment. Besides, I want to try out The Wicked Horse. You've talked about it so much that I've got to give it a go. Got to see my machine in practical action."

"You'll love it," I say without any enthusiasm.

"You sure you're okay?" he asks again. This time, his words are sober with concern.

"I'm fine, Micah. Just a long day and longer night. I'll talk to you soon, buddy."

"Okay. Take care."

I disconnect the phone and tap it against my chin for a moment before I pull the photos up again. I take in every detail of her that I can see, but I mostly concentrate on the close up of the dildo sliding into her. I tear my eyes away only for a moment so I can bend over the side of my bed to snatch my jeans. I pull the pair of panties I'd stowed there earlier tonight, bringing them to my nose as I settle back against the headboard. I inhale her scent deeply, and I'm consumed with lust.

My hand reaches below the sheet and palms my cock with the silk of her panties in between. My dick goes harder as I focus on Jorie's ass. It's phenomenal, and I'd love to fuck it while she's riding that dildo.

A bolt of pleasure over the thought slams through me, and I squeeze my shaft hard. I have to back it down and quit thinking like that.

That is never going to happen.

Jorie and I are never going to happen again.

I have not beaten off to the thought of Jorie once since I found her in the bathroom that night, bleeding from fending off her attackers. That night made it clear she was too innocent to be dominating my dirty thoughts. When she turned eighteen and moved away to go to school at UCLA, we lost touch because the only contact I ever really had with her was as a neighbor and Micah's little sister. I kept up to speed on her through Micah and accepted what he chose to share. I never asked.

I didn't go to her wedding because I didn't want to see how gorgeous she'd be in a snowy-white gown, looking with adoration at her soon-to-be husband.

I had put Jorie firmly out of my mind as the years went by.

Staring at the photo as I stroke myself, I remember how good she felt in my arms. I think about those green eyes locking to mine as I drove into her over and over again.

I vow to myself I'll have this one last happy with Jorie Pearce in mind, and then I'm going to let her go just the way I did before.

CHAPTER 6

Jorie

ELENA SAID THIS could be a bad idea. But, in fairness, she thought it could be a freaking amazing idea, too. I'm choosing to go with the "amazing idea" theory because I just can't leave things the way we did. I can't stop thinking of the way Walsh made me feel. And I'm not talking just pleasure. I'm talking about the fact that he made me feel gorgeous and revered. I felt sexy as hell with him, and I don't remember feeling that way for a very long time. He peeled back a layer of my metaphorical sexual onion. It feels raw and awkwardly new, and I need to figure out what to do with it.

I also need to figure out what to do with Walsh.

He was clearly horrified to have inadvertently crossed a line with me, but when I woke up this morning, I had to think to myself… so what? It wasn't intentional, and even if it was, there is no fault because we did nothing wrong. We're both adults and free to make those choices.

So my visit to The Royale, which is Walsh's hotel

and casino, is to make sure he's okay and isn't wallowing in regret. Walsh and Micah are as tight as blood brothers. It would stand to reason Walsh feels the "bro code" has been violated. As such, my purpose here is to make sure his guilt is assuaged and he doesn't feel bad about supposedly betraying Micah.

I stare up at the monstrous building made of chrome and glass, trying ignore my conscience sneering at me.

Okay, who am I kidding? I'm here because I want more of Walsh. Vince may have dinged my self-esteem when it comes to my sexual prowess, but he didn't damage my overall ego. There's enough of it left intact, coupled with the fact Walsh has awoken something within me that I simply want more of.

Squaring my shoulders, I march into The Royale and head straight for the concierge desk. I haven't been in this casino before. Hell, I haven't been in hardly any of them. Sure, I'd only grown up about forty-five minutes away, but gambling and all-you-can-eat buffets held no interest to me.

From Micah bragging about his best friend over the years, I knew Walsh orchestrated the purchase of the land, then pulled together financing with two other partners to build this casino. It's one of the most popular on the strip, boasting five-star dining, old-world elegance, and superior customer service. Again, all this from Micah, but honestly… I'm so proud of Walsh, too. We may have lost touch over the years, but I'll never forget all the ways in which he acted as a big brother to me.

Ick.

Okay… that's gross. Thinking of Walsh like a brother.

I scrub my mind clean of that thought and demand myself never to do that again.

Rather, I'll never forget all the ways in which Walsh provided me friendship and support in my formative years.

Yes… much better.

"Can I help you?" a man behind the concierge desk asks with a genuine and friendly smile. Not snooty as I would expect in a fancy hotel, and I guess that goes to the superior customer service The Royale strives for.

"Yes… hi," I say as I nervously tuck my hair behind my ears on both sides. "I need to see Mr. Brooks. How do I go about getting access to his apartment?"

Micah told me some time ago that Walsh lives here.

The concierge never loses his friendly smile, but a single eyebrow arches high at my temerity.

"Oh, gosh," I stammer. "That came out stalkerish. Mr. Brooks… I mean, Walsh… and I are longtime friends. He used to babysit me."

"Your name?" the man asks as he pulls up something on his computer.

"Jorie Pearce."

After a moment of scanning, he looks up at me.

"Your name isn't on the approved list."

"Well, he's not exactly expecting me."

"I'm sorry, Miss Pearce," he says with true regret in his voice. "But our policy is strict. No one gets up to the private penthouse without their name on the list."

I lean on the desk with one elbow and lower my voice. "Just out of curiosity… are there any women on that list?"

The eyebrow shoots up again.

"No, wait," I say hastily as I hold my palms toward him in a silent plea to not process my last request either mentally or on the computer. "That's totally stalkerish, and I didn't mean that."

"Miss Pearce," the concierge says, now with a hint of annoyance. "Perhaps you'd like to leave a message? I can get it up to Mr. Brooks today and he can call you."

"No, I need to see him now," I tell him firmly. "And I swear it's not to cook a rabbit in a pot on his stove. Can you please just call up to his apartment?"

"That's not our policy—"

"Look," I snap as I lean across the desk slightly. "I'm a lifelong friend of Walsh's. My brother is his best friend. We lost touch for a few years, but we ran into each other last night. I really need to talk to him about something that happened last night, and I'm not leaving this hotel until you call up to his apartment."

The eyebrow doesn't arch but it does draw inward to meet its match on the other side as he considers what I just said.

"I swear to you," and here I pause to look at his name tag, "Bentley. Please just call him. He won't be mad."

With a sigh, he relents and picks up the phone receiver, punching in a five-digit number. After a pause, he says, "Mr. Brooks… I'm very sorry to disturb you, sir, but there's a Miss Jorie Pearce here to see you. She says she's a longtime friend."

I watch as Bentley listens, but I can't gauge what's being said as his face remains blank. Finally, he says, "Very good, sir."

I take this to mean I'll be getting an escort to the penthouse suite, but Bentley replaces the receiver and says, "I'm sorry, Miss Pearce. But Mr. Walsh told me to tell you he's busy and can't receive you right now."

My eyes narrow at Bentley. "I don't believe you. Call back and let me talk to him."

"I assure you, I just talked to him and that's what he said."

"Call him back," I order as I point to the phone.

"I can't," he says almost with a wail. "If I do, he'll fire me."

Okay, that hits home. I don't want to get anyone in trouble, so I say, "Fine. Give me just a moment."

I take a few steps away from the concierge desk and pull my iPhone out. I shoot off a quick text to Micah. *What's Walsh's phone number?*

I wait a few moments, but I know Micah is awake in San Francisco at this hour. His phone is always on, and he never ignores a text from me.

He responds with the number before I can even start to tap my foot with impatience, adding on, *Why?*

I hate the lie, but I write back, *Came to Vegas for the day. Thought I'd see if he could meet up for lunch. Haven't seen him in years.*

Cool, he writes back. *Tell him I said, "what's up, douche?"*

I roll my eyes as I text back, *Real mature. Love ya. Later.*

After I save the number to my contacts, I open a new text to Walsh. *Let me up to see you or I'm going straight back to The Wicked Horse to satisfy some further curiosities I have.*

I hit send and then walk back to the concierge desk. I merely lean one elbow on it and watch Bentley with a silent smile. The phone rings about ten seconds after that.

Bentley's eyes fly to mine as he listens, and then says, "Yes, sir. Right away."

When he replaces the receiver, he says, "I'm to show you to the penthouse elevator."

"Thank you, Bentley," I say brightly.

He scurries out from behind his desk, and I follow him through the main floor of the casino to a locked door that he opens with a security card. This leads to an elevator that opens when he pushes a button, and then with another swipe of his card on the interior, he pushes a button that says Penthouse Suite.

Nice.

Bentley gives me a smile before he backs out of the elevator and the doors close.

I have no clue how tall The Royale is, but I'm guessing twenty floors or so. The ride up is swift, though, as there are no floors underneath to stop at.

When the doors open, I'm momentarily stunned to be looking at a living room, as I hadn't expected the elevator to open right into Walsh's apartment.

"This better be good, Jorie," Walsh growls, and I turn to see him laying on a couch to my left with a tennis ball in his hand. He tosses the ball up casually and catches it. He tilts his head my way, one leg laying straight, the other propped up casually.

And wow… he looks good in casual. Just a pair of track pants and a t-shirt that's not overly tight but fits his form nicely. His feet are bare and the top half of his long hair is pulled back in a ponytail.

"What are you doing?" I ask instead. "Brooding?"

"Not in the mood for your sass," he mutters as he sits up and puts the tennis ball on the coffee table. He plants both feet on the ground and props his elbows on his thighs to watch me with a flat expression. "Had enough of it during your tween years."

"Stop it," I say swiftly.

"Stop what?"

"Stop talking about me as if I'm a kid to you," I tell him.

"But for the years I was around you, you were a kid," he reminds me. "That's how I remember you best."

"Liar," I say softly as I walk toward him. "You remember me best by what we did last night."

Walsh's jaw tightens as he watches me come closer.

"I'm curious," I continue as I come to a stop on the other side of the coffee table. "Had you ever thought about me in a dirty way before last night?"

A muscle starts jumping right where his jaw meets his ear. The flash of guilt in his eyes and his silence tells me he did. A flood of triumph and desire courses through me as I realize that last night wasn't just a fluke.

"Walsh," I say as I take a step around the coffee table.

"Don't," he snaps at me as he stands swiftly from the couch and moves the opposite way to keep the table between us. "Just don't come near me."

I blink at him in surprise. For a moment, I think I might have made an unwise decision. Maybe Vince did more damage to my self-esteem than I had originally thought, because my first reaction is Walsh is keeping me at bay because last night was a fluke and he's repulsed by me.

I flush with embarrassment and take two steps backward. "Um… I think I might have—"

"Christ," Walsh snarls as he rounds the coffee table

and takes me by my shoulders. "Don't get it in your head that you did anything wrong last night. I can see it written all over your face. You are the sexiest thing I think I've ever laid my eyes on, but Jorie… you and I are not going to happen again. Ever."

"I'm the sexiest thing you've ever laid eyes on, but you don't want me?" I ask with uncertainty because I am beyond confused.

Walsh closes his eyes briefly, taking a deep breath in that flares his nostrils wide. When he releases it, his eyes open to pin me in place. "You are Micah's little sister and I just can't."

"But that's stupid—"

"It's not," he says softly but with absolute surety.

"I don't get it. You'll have to do better than that because we are both adults. I need a better explanation, Walsh, because what we did last night… I never—"

"Just don't," he snaps again as he spins away. "I don't need the reminder."

"Was it bad?" I ask, because that's the way he's acting right this moment. Good God, he's confusing the shit out of me.

Walsh looks over his shoulders at me, shooting me an exasperated look. "That's about the dumbest question you've ever asked me, and trust me… you had some stupid ones growing up."

I take my own deep breath, trying to calm my nerves and my annoyance. "Okay… please just tell me why me being Micah's sister should stop us from having a relationship?"

"I don't do relationships," he says icily. "Only no-strings fucking."

"I'm down with that," I say with a shrug. Truly that's not really the way I operate as I'm more of a traditional girl, but hey… my husband kicked me out of our house so maybe I need to reevaluate my personal norms.

"God, Jorie," Walsh says with a pleading voice. "Why can't you just accept—"

"I'll accept it if you give me a good reason, Walsh," I tell him with sincerity. "Just take a few moments and explain it to me. We're both adults."

"Fine," he says as he jerks his head toward a chair that sits adjacent to the couch. I take a seat there as he silently requested. He sits back down on the couch, elbows on his knees as he looks me right in the eye. "Micah is more than my best friend. He's like a brother to me."

"I get that," I say quickly. "Your parents did more raising of him than my dad did."

Walsh nods. "But that's not the only reason, Jorie. I watched *you* grow up. No, I more than watched. I had a hand in helping you to grow up. Every time Micah had to watch you, I was there, too. I watched you learn to crawl and then walk. I watched you get scraped knees, play with dolls, and score soccer goals. Christ, you even made Micah and me have tea parties with you. Then I watched you develop into a beautiful girl who crushed on boys along with Elena. I watched your heart get broken, and I beat two guys who hurt you to bloody pulps. Yes, Micah's like a brother to me, but Jorie… you're like a sister, and I just can't."

Complete disappointment floods through me as I had not considered this at all. I thought this was a bro thing, which I can argue against all day long. Micah would never begrudge me a relationship with Walsh, assuming Walsh was open to one. He has made me question that, but first…

"When was the first time you had a dirty thought about me?" I ask, changing the conversation to throw him a little off balance.

Never in my life have I seen Walsh embarrassed. First, it would be hard to tell given his olive skin—passed down to him by his Greek mother—but second… Walsh is just one of the most self-possessed people I know. He doesn't blush.

Except right now, I can see red clearly staining his cheeks.

"When?" I press upon him.

"Doesn't matter," he says as he stands abruptly from the couch. "You wanted an explanation and I gave it to you. I need you to accept it and move on from this, Jorie. What happened last night was amazing. You're amazing and Vince is wrong about you. But it's not going to be me who helps you along this journey of self-discovery. It can't be me."

I don't stand right away, but merely study him for a moment so I can assess how strongly he believes his own words. Judging by the hard set to his jaw and the concrete determination focused right on me, I'm guessing he believes it deeply.

"Fine," I say as I stand up and walk toward the elevator. "I just hope it's not awkward if we run into each other at The Wicked Horse again."

"It won't be," he grits out, the muscle in his cheek jumping again.

Hmm… I thought that little threat might get him to budge, but he's calling my supposed bluff.

Here's the thing, though. Walsh hasn't seen me for a long time. I've grown in ways he'd have no idea about. He's judging me based on an image of a little girl.

What he doesn't know is that I don't bluff. If I say I'm going to do something, I do it.

I give him a bright smile as I step backward into the elevator and push the one and only button available. "Good. But if you're in any way anxious about it, I'd avoid The Orgy Room tonight. That's the room I want to try out next."

The doors slide shut, and I smile at the fury on Walsh's face.

CHAPTER 7

Walsh

I'VE BEEN COMING to The Wicked Horse ever since it opened a little over two years ago. I forged an easy friendship with its owner, Jerico, and it absolutely suits my lifestyle.

For as long as I've been sexually active, I've always been dirty.

I mean, really dirty.

My ex-wife Renee can attest to that, and it was really the one thing that held the marriage together for as long as it did. She was a wildcat in bed. While The Wicked Horse wasn't around when we were together, she would have totally been a swinger there with me. I know this because we swung with other couples on occasion.

Once I got divorced, I found dating to be just fucking hard. It was more effort than it was worth. I didn't want to get married again, but not because Renee destroyed me or anything. In fact, our parting was quite amicable. It's just that marriage didn't serve any purpose.

At least my marriage to Renee hadn't other than having constant and amazing sex whenever I wanted it. After my divorce, I wasn't lonely. I didn't feel the need to share my deepest thoughts with a woman. I was completely fine and happy having casual sex without commitments.

So coming to The Wicked Horse has always been a treat. It's never been repetitive. It's never been dull. It's been quite fulfilling as a matter of fact, which is probably why I come at least five out of seven days of the week.

But tonight, as I ride the elevator up, my stomach is cramped into a painful knot. I'm here two hours earlier than I normally come, and only because I need to know if Jorie is really going to take advantage of this place again.

I swear I'm not going to interfere, but I need to know.

"Good evening, Mr. Brooks," Larissa says from behind the podium with a welcoming smile. She's a great fuck, and I've had her multiple times. I'm not the kind of man who only has a woman once. If she's sweet and makes me come, I'll hit it again.

And again.

I just won't buy her dinner for it first.

"Larissa," I say somewhat stiffly because I'm tense as hell. I should ask her to take a break and suck my cock, but that wouldn't even scratch the surface of my anxiety.

I head to the bar and order two fingers of whiskey, house brand being fine because I do nothing more than shoot it down. The bartender eyes me warily since I never drink alcohol here. With a hiss, I set the glass down and make my way to The Orgy Room to see if Jorie is really going to do what she promised.

♦

Two hours later, she still hasn't shown, and I don't know whether I'm relieved or pissed. I mean... of course I'm relieved she's not here. I don't want her randomly fucking guys because she needs to prove to her ex-douche that she's sexy and desirable. I'm happy she hasn't walked through those doors.

But I am slightly pissed I've wasted two hours of my life because I let Jorie pull my chain.

No, wait... she *yanked* my chain and she did it hard.

She did it to prove I'm invested in her and she did it brilliantly, little minx. I have it in my mind that the next time I see her, I should bend her over my lap and turn that pale skin bright red with the palm of my hand.

No, wait... not going to see her again. We're done. If I were to put her over my lap and spank her, that would most definitely lead to me slipping a finger inside to see how much she loved it and then that would lead to us tearing each other up.

I'm sure of it.

My eyes roam around The Orgy Room where I've been waiting for Jorie to appear. There's a chance, I suppose, she went to one of the other rooms to seek her pleasure, but I doubt it. She mentioned this room specifically because the little smartass knew I'd show. Her not showing means she has the power right now, and I don't like that one bit. Control is my middle name.

I should just fuck someone in here. There's not a woman in here who would say "no" to me and I've had several approach who I've turned down. Pick a girl, pound one out for both of us, and get gone. Easy plan.

Except I've sat here in this room for almost two hours, watching all kinds of filthy stuff going on, and while my dick isn't dead, it hasn't reacted appropriately. It's been semi-hard for sure, but it's not been aching for release. I have a moment of panic that maybe I'm getting too old for this shit, or that I'm just not turned on by this stuff anymore, which means my sex life will be on the decline.

But I immediately push that thought away. I have no choice but to because Jorie struts into The Orgy Room, and my dick goes rock hard. She's wearing a denim miniskirt that's barely covering her goods, black ankle boots with a heel so high I'm not sure how she walks, and a white halter top that's so thin her hard nipples are poking through.

Fuck.

I involuntarily push my palm down onto my dick, not to rearrange it, but to try to force it into submission.

No luck.

Her eyes scan the room slowly... leisurely. They

cross over me, and she sees me standing there because she gives me a slight smile and a nod of greeting before continuing her perusal. She doesn't look back my way, and that fucking pisses me off so badly my feet are moving before my brain tells them to.

As I cross the room, Jorie's eyes seem to focus on something, so I look that way.

A man, lounging provocatively on one of the couches, beckons her closer. She smiles at him and moves his way.

Oh, hell no.

I cut across toward her on the diagonal, hurdling one of the low chaises to stand in front of her ten feet before she reaches the guy.

"Not going to happen," I tell her firmly as she's brought up short.

Jorie smiles up at me, and that black hair with her bangs right over those green eyes makes a startling effect. They remind me of the snake in *The Jungle Book*, the way it hypnotized that little boy. Jorie used to make Micah and me watch that with her over and over again. I hated that stupid movie but right now, the memories make me want to smile.

"Good," she says as she steps in close to me, placing a hand on my stomach. "You've come to your senses."

Christ, it kills me, but I take her hand in mine and push it gently off. "My senses are the same as they were this morning. Nothing's changed. You're just not going to be using this club to get your rocks off."

"Well, that's fine if you don't feel any differently," Jorie says calmly and makes a move to step around me. "But you have no control over me. I can do whatever I want in this club."

Fury rages through me that she's so cavalier about this. She doesn't seem put out at all that I'm not interested in her that way, but that rage is nothing compared to what I feel at the thought of some random dude putting his hands on her.

"Jorie," I warn, and I swear it's the same tone I used once when she was little and was getting ready to touch the outdoor grill my dad was cooking on.

She turns fully to me, and I can't help but notice the way her breasts sway under the material of her top as she does. I want to fucking bite them.

"You can either fuck me or I'm getting it from someone else tonight," she says resolutely.

My cock is jumping up and down yelling, *Pick me, pick me.* "I don't think of you that way."

Jorie rolls her eyes because she knows that's as ludicrous a statement as it sounds.

"But you have thought of me that way," she says, reminding me of something that shames me greatly. Tilting her head slightly, she asks, "Tell me, Walsh... how old was I? What was your dirty thought?"

I don't answer. I refuse to answer.

"Want to know a secret?" she asks.

I keep my mouth firmly clamped shut.

She leans in and whispers. "I've had dirty thoughts about you before… when I was younger. Lots of them actually."

My balls start tingling. She thought of me that way before?

"Back when I first started, um… discovering things about my body," she continues in a husky tone. "When I'd lay in bed at night and touch myself."

Jesus fuck.

Her eyes study me carefully, waiting to see some reaction. I don't show it, though. I don't let her see I want her so badly that I'd sell my soul to the devil right now just sink to my cock an inch inside her pussy. Clamping down hard on my conscience for stability, I refuse to let myself be baited into something I'll regret again, no matter how good it will feel getting to that regret.

Realizing she's not getting the reaction she wants, she gives a nonchalant shrug and sidesteps me, her intent to head to the man she was originally walking toward.

I turn and watch her take a step, then another.

One more, and I'm filled with a dire urgency to prevent her from doing this.

No… filled with a need to prevent her from doing this with anyone but me.

It only takes me two paces before I've got her hand locked in mine. She gives a small gasp as I pull her in the opposite direction toward the exit door.

"What are you doing?" she asks as she tries to pull away.

"I'm taking you back to my place." I give a tug on her so she catches up to my long stride. "And I don't want to hear anything from you about it. You want me to fuck you? Fine, but it's going to be done in privacy."

She doesn't say a word, so I keep muttering. "Can't believe you came to a sex club, for fuck's sake. Or came back to one a second time. Jesus, Jorie… just… fuck."

I think I hear her husky laugh and I swear I'd strangle her if it was true, but I grit my teeth and don't say another word as we make our way back to the Social Room.

"Call down and have them bring my car around," I tell Larissa.

"Yes, Mr. Brooks," she says as I punch the elevator button. The doors immediately open, and we walk in. Jorie stands close to me on the ride down. Maybe I'm going crazy or something, but I feel like I can smell her lust. Or maybe it's mine I'm smelling.

We reach the bottom floor, through the lobby of the Onyx Casino, and for the first time, I leave The Wicked Horse with a hard-on. My car is indeed waiting for me, and my driver opens the door. With my hand gently on Jorie's back, I guide her in first. She moves to the opposite side. When I get in, I stick to my side, knowing if I touch her, I'll fuck her before we make it back to The

Royale.

In fact, I don't even look at her.

She's too much of a temptation.

CHAPTER 8

Jorie

I'M SLIGHTLY DISAPPOINTED that Walsh pulled me out of The Wicked Horse. The sexual energy in that place is off the charts, and I want to do very bad things with him in front of a lot of people.

But I can't be too disappointed when I'm ultimately getting what I wanted, which is Walsh. He might be like my older brother in some ways, but not in enough to deter me the way it's deterring him. I've crushed on the man since I knew what a crush was, and I wasn't lying when I said I had dirty thoughts about him. But we went our separate ways, and I forgot about him in those sexy ways.

Until last night when he had me in The Wicked Horse, and now it might be fair to say I'm obsessed with feeling that way again. Yes, we were in a public place and yes, he had me on a freaking dildo machine, but truth be told… it was all Walsh who made me feel so good. I may not have known it was *him* behind that mask, but I certainly was drawn to many things about the mysterious man. His physical looks, his magnetic presence, and his completely alpha orders to me were exactly what I was craving.

Vince was not like that in bed. If anything, he was sort of passive and unsure of himself at times the more I think about it. Well, the more I compare him to Walsh. Maybe I wasn't any good with him because he didn't give me any reason to be?

The ride to The Royale is done in silence because I'm afraid that one mistaken word from me will have Walsh simply driving me to Henderson and dumping me off at my apartment. I know I've pushed him to his limits and I've goaded him into something that he feels is wrong, but ultimately my conscience can handle that for two reasons.

First, he's a big boy and he had a choice. He chose me.

Second, he might think it's wrong, but I'm positive he wants me very badly so I'm really doing him a solid.

Right?

Our car pulls up to the front of The Royale. Walsh opens the door and steps out without waiting for the driver. He's pissed at me so I'm surprised when he offers me his hand to exit. I do so, tugging my skirt back down. I'd dressed totally appropriate for The Wicked Horse, but not so much to walk through an elegant hotel.

I try to press into him as we walk into the lobby, but

he steps a bit away from me as he mutters, "You dressed the part to seduce me tonight, Jor. Own it."

My face flames hot as we walk hand in hand to the private elevator that will lead up to his penthouse. He doesn't have a security card to swipe the way Bentley did, but he flips open a panel and punches in a long code.

Walsh watches me with hard eyes as he stands opposite of me, and I can't decide if I should try to lessen his anger. Part of me thinks not, because there's a part of me that's excited to see what he'll do with it.

When the elevator doors open, Walsh extends his hand in a silent invitation for me to precede him into the living area. I do and make it no more than five steps before he says, "Stop."

I do and turn around to look at him. My jaw drops and my heart starts racing as I see him slide his belt free of his slacks. There's a low-burning flame in his eyes and a hard set to his jaw.

"Did you ever drop to your knees to welcome your husband home from work?" he asks as he drops the belt to the floor and undoes the button to his pants.

"What?" I ask in stunned surprise.

"Come on, Jorie," he taunts me as he slips the zipper down. "You went to a sex club last night looking for answers. You've set out to discover something about your sexuality. So, tell me… are you the type of woman who will take her lover's cock down her throat when he walks in the door? Willing to get some rug burns on your knees when he fucks your face?"

Oh, wow.

Holy shit.

That is hot as all get out, and my sex spasms.

I don't answer Walsh because, sadly, I have never done that with Vince. It never crossed my mind, and I think it never did because I never craved him. Or perhaps he never was that great in giving me pleasure, so I didn't ever want to return it. Or maybe it was the fact that he was an asshole a lot of the time, so I really didn't think he deserved it.

But my mouth floods with saliva as Walsh takes his dick out and strokes it slowly while he watches me. I don't hesitate. I walk right to him and drop to my knees.

That gorgeous cock looms huge in front of me, a clear bead of pre-cum on the tip. I lean forward to touch it with my tongue, but his hand comes out to stop me. A thumb goes under my chin, his fingers curling around the side of my neck.

"I don't want you to lick me," he says roughly. "Or suck me. I want to fuck your mouth. Do you understand there's a difference?"

I shake my head, and I'm so turned on now by his words I want to put my hand between my legs.

"You will when I'm finished with you," he says darkly. "Then you might think twice about goading me."

"If you're trying to scare me," I tell him, twisting my neck so he releases his hold. "It won't work. I'm not leaving."

"Damn right you're not leaving," he returns with a growl. "But I want you to see that just because we're not in The Wicked Horse, it doesn't mean it's not going to be kinky, dirty fucking. You might be playing with a fire you can't handle."

"I'll take the ri—" I start to say, but then his cock is in my mouth with his hands on both sides of my head to hold me in place.

He slides in slowly, pushing to deliberately test my gag reflex, and it kicks in the minute the head touches the back of my tongue. Walsh backs out just as slowly, but never leaves my mouth.

Staring down at me with glittering, lust-filled eyes, he murmurs, "I don't mind you leaking a few uncomfortable tears to take me down, but I don't want you gagging. Try swallowing this time."

God… how can I be so turned on when he's talking about making me uncomfortable to the point of tears?

I give him a nod, and he slowly pushes in as his gaze stays locked to where we're connected.

"Been dying to get that cherry lipstick on my cock," he says in such a soft voice I can barely hear him.

My own hand involuntarily starts to dive under my skirt, but he gives me a harsh, "Don't. You only get off by my hand, tongue, or dick, got it?"

I nod again, and as the head of his cock starts to hit that area that will make me gag, I work my throat in a valiant effort to take him down.

And I gag again, harder than the last time.

Walsh immediately pulls all the way out and gives me a chastising shake of his head. "You might want to practice this in the future, but for right now, I know your limits."

I lick my lower lip and patiently wait for him to give it to me again. I try not to be disheartened by the fact he said *I* would have to practice, not *we* would have to practice.

His hands tightening their hold on my head, he pushes his hips forward and enters my mouth for a third time. I sheath my teeth, concentrate on stroking him with my tongue and the roof of my mouth, and adding on a tiny bit of a sucking motion. This lasts about ten seconds because he starts to move a little more roughly, never quite getting deep enough to gag me, but making it a little difficult to keep my tongue and lips in sync with his thrusts.

Faster he goes, and I give up trying to pleasure him with my own moves. I can do nothing more than let him use my mouth as a vessel and as he starts to hammer into me, my saliva is leaking out past my lips.

"That's it," he praises me, but I don't know what I've done other than slobber.

I suck in air through my nose because he's so large in my mouth it's the only way I can breathe. His breathing is getting rougher, and he starts to encroach on the back of my mouth the harder he fucks my face. He's going so fast I don't even have time to gag, but I'm surprised when tears fill my eyes as he promised. I'm not being hurt in any way, but I am being used roughly. If the wetness in my panties is any indication, I love it.

Walsh starts cursing under his breath. I blink my eyes rapidly, letting the tears spill down my cheeks, and look up to find him staring at me in such a way my pussy starts to cramp with my own need. His jaw is locked hard, teeth gritted, and I can tell he's on the brink of coming. It's the sexiest look I've ever seen on another human being, and I find myself anticipating his release.

"Fuck," Walsh barks out. He goes still in my mouth, the head of his cock resting in the middle of my tongue, and he starts to unload. God, he even tastes good. Not bitter but mellow, and my throat starts working to take it all from him.

"Fuck," he says again, this time on a satisfied moan as he slowly pulls out. His gaze softens slightly as he looks down at his dick. "I knew that red lipstick would look good on me."

My eyes slide to his cock, which is still looking impressive in size, and I have no clue what my mouth looks like but I'm sure most of my lipstick is gone. It's smeared beautifully along the length of his shaft.

I'm shocked when Walsh drops to his knees and his mouth crashes against mine. He kisses me hard without asking for entrance, taking control of my tongue and laying final claim to ownership of my mouth.

He pulls back just enough to whisper, "Greedy girl. Can't taste myself."

I can do nothing but moan over his words. Then his lips come to my cheek and he kisses my tears, using the tip of his tongue to take a tiny taste. "Your tears taste fucking good, Jorie."

"Walsh," I whisper, now in sensory overload.

He just taught me what it meant to fuck a face, and now I know the difference. Watching how he handled me roughly and how turned on he was as he did it has made me so sensitive between my legs, it's not going to take much to make me climax.

With surprising grace, Walsh stands up and brings me right along with him. Not even bothering to tuck his half-hard dick back in his pants, he takes me by the hand and leads me through his enormous and quite lavishly decorated apartment. I didn't notice it too much the first time I was here, and I'm certainly only able to get a cursory look right now, but the man has no problem spending money as far as I can see.

Walsh heads through an open kitchen to a hallway that leads straight back to his bedroom. He gives me a little push to my back. "Get naked and get on the bed."

I don't hesitate. I'm all for getting past the awkward removal of clothes. He has to be well sated right this moment, but his eyes burn no less hot than before he came in my mouth. He watches as I shimmy out of my clothes, but I look right back at him as he disrobes. We did the dirtiest type of fucking one can do last night, and we've never seen each other naked.

Walsh doesn't disappoint. His torso is as fabulous as I remembered but it's only complemented by his muscular legs and tight ass. He's perfectly built in my opinion, but I might be a little biased. I've loved this man since I was a little girl, only in a familial/friendship type way, but I've also thought about him in other ways, too. The sight of his naked body, even as his dick is softening, makes me achy with need for him.

"Bed, Jorie," Walsh reminds me.

I crawl on it with the intent to lay in a sexy pose as I turn over to face Walsh, but he's on the bed with me quick as lightning and flipping me to my back to straddle me right at my pelvis.

I use the opportunity to check his package out better. It's still large even in its softened state and he keeps himself trimmed tight, which I love. My eyes go up to find him staring at my tits.

"They don't bite," I say jokingly, and his gaze comes to meet mine.

His lips curve slightly. "But I do. It's probably going to hurt a little."

A shudder ripples through me, and my nipples harden. Walsh's eyes flick back down to my breasts. "Look at that. Looks like they want to be bitten."

I swallow hard and wait with anticipation for him to

lay torture upon then. My nipples have never been supersensitive so the thought of him getting a little rough with them is thrilling.

"But I want something else first," Walsh says, and I blink my eyes to focus back on him. He moves backward, pushing his knees down in between my legs so they spread.

There's no hesitation, only hungry determination as he lays down and pushes his face into my pussy. My back arches off the bed at the feel of his mouth on me. There's no teasing movements, and he hits my clit hard and fast.

It only takes seconds before I'm screaming out his name as he gives me my first orgasm of the night.

CHAPTER 9

Walsh

I CAN'T REMEMBER the last time I woke up with a woman in my bed. Of course, women have stayed over since Renee and I divorced three years ago after just one year of marriage as I don't use The Wicked Horse exclusively for my needs. I've brought women up here before, fucked them, and fallen asleep. I've got nothing against cuddling, and I certainly like the benefits of having a warm pussy to slide into first thing in the morning.

But Jorie's soft body spooned against mine isn't like anything I've felt before. I not only know her body intimately after all we did last night, but I also know *her* intimately. More intimately than I've ever known a woman, and it makes all the difference in the world waking up to her beside me.

Jorie's twenty-eight, and I was eight when she was born. I've known her a long fucking time, and I'd be a liar to deny I care about her. But having a relationship with her isn't doable in my opinion. First, I've no desire to get married again. Don't really want kids. Those are things women want for the most part, and I could never offer that to her.

But more importantly, Micah won't accept it. He'll view it as wrong as I do, given our almost-familial ties. I know this because Micah got a hint of my feelings about Jorie once when I was drunk, and he went berserk. He made no bones about the fact she was off limits to me because Micah viewed me as his brother, and he also viewed me as Jorie's brother, too. The fuck of it is, Jorie's right... I do find the whole forbidden little sister angle dirty and taboo. I'm going straight to hell, but that makes it more exciting.

Keeping it hidden from Micah won't make it exciting, though. It's dangerous and a serious blow to the loyalty and trust he has in me.

Even knowing all this, it didn't stop me from having her repeatedly last night.

Doesn't stop me from wanting her right now as evidenced by the extreme morning wood I've got going on planted right in the crease of her ass cheeks. The thought of popping her anal cherry makes me go even harder. Last night, I'd learned she'd never done that, so I made it my mission to introduce her ass to my tongue and fingers so she'd start to get used to it.

Christ, I've got to stop thinking in terms of fucking her again. This should be it. *The end. Done. Move on.*

Don't look back.

If we can do that, Micah will stay in the dark and I'll eventually get over this guilt.

Jorie starts to wake, pressing back into me, wiggling her ass a little as she gives a tiny yawn. My hand, which had been resting on her hip, digs down into her flesh to hold her still.

She gives a sexy little laugh and wiggles again. Her voice is raw and husky as she says, "Good morning to you, too."

I need to shut this down. Get her out of here.

Giving her hip a tiny pat, I say casually, "I'll fix you breakfast, then you can be on your way."

"Oh, Walsh," Jorie says with slight exasperation. Her hand takes mine from her hip and drags it down in between her legs. "There's only one thing I'm hungry for right now."

Christ. I can't say no to this, not when my fingers dip inside of her, coaxing her to slippery arousal. She moans and circles her hips, causing my cock to slip down in between her legs.

One last time, then it's done.

Jorie groans as I start to circle her clit with her own moisture. Her head presses back into my shoulder, her pelvis flexing and tilting, which drags the length of my cock through her pussy lips. She's slippery as fuck already and I start to thrust against her slowly, doing nothing more than coating my hard shaft with her juices.

Taking my hand away from her clit, Jorie slides it up to her breast so I can pinch at her nipple. I learned last night that she likes the rough handling, and they've got to be sore as fuck today. Still, she moans harder as I twist one and her hips buck backward in a silent plea for me.

I thrust faster in between her legs, still doing nothing more than running myself through her pussy lips. I bet I could get off this way.

I'm so lost to the sensation it takes me a moment to realize Jorie's got her hand between her legs, meeting the tip of my cock when it pushes through from behind. She tilts her hips, trying to push it inside of her.

"Jorie," I chastise her roughly. "Let me get a condom."

"No," she says, and just the thought that she wants me inside of her causes my hips to tilt at an angle that will let me thrust upward if I so choose.

But I stop in place, my cock practically pulsing with the need to sink in.

"Birth control?" I ask.

She rotates her hips, trying to drag me in, and gives a little grunt of frustration before she gasps. "Pill."

Fuck. I thrust hard upward and sink right into her slippery channel. She cries out and her muscles tighten all around me, and Jesus… I need to come like right now.

I roll and shove Jorie onto her stomach, and she gasps when I haul her up to her hands and knees, my cock still planted in deep from behind.

Fucking amazing.

My bare cock being squeezed by Jorie's warm cunt has got to be the best thing in forever.

I start fucking her roughly, my balls swinging to slap at her pussy so hard they hurt. But I don't care. Her ass jiggles as it slaps against my pelvis, and Jorie's moaning urges me on harder. My hands grip tight to her hips, and she rocks against me as her back arches from the pleasure.

"I won't ever fucking get enough of this," I admit foolishly through gritted teeth, and I know Jorie will never let that go. She'll hold that against me later.

My only hope is she's so lost in the throes of passion that she didn't hear it.

An orgasm starts to brew, causing my balls to contract. My ass muscles are cramping from how fast and hard I'm fucking Jorie, and she's practically sobbing beneath me in pleasure. It's only when she screams and starts to shake with her own release that I give into it, slamming in hard and releasing my all into her.

"God, Jorie… fuck," I mutter as I grind against her ass.

I haven't come in a woman in a long time. Not since Renee, but I don't remember it being this good. I don't remember it feeling so satisfying knowing that a woman's pussy is filled with my cum. I feel like I've marked Jorie in some way, and I'm afraid that means I'm not kicking her out of my bed anytime soon.

♦

"I'll take some breakfast now," Jorie says from underneath me. I'd collapsed there moments after coming so hard I saw lights flickering under my eyelids, but I'd been holding most of my weight off her.

"In a little bit," I groan as I roll off her and come to rest on my side.

She stays on her stomach and merely twists her head to look at me. "I'm starving."

"I'm broken," I mutter. "Give a man time to recuperate."

And then Jorie grins at me, her lush lips completely devoid of that bright red lipstick, yet she has mascara smeared under her eyes. Her hair is all tangled with what looks like a bird's nest on one side of her head. She looks like a sexy siren who has been fucking all night, and yet she looks just like the Jorie I've always known.

"Will you tell me now?" she asks softly.

"Tell you what?"

"When was the first time you had a dirty thought about me?"

I stare at her a moment, recalling the memory as clear as day. While my dick is indeed a little broken right now, the thought of fifteen-year-old Jorie in a bathing suit still causes lust to stir within me.

"I was home visiting my parents for a weekend." She

lifts to her elbows, head still tilted my way as she listens. "I could see you in the backyard sunbathing."

"You mean burning," she says.

Chuckling, I tell her, "You hadn't been out there long. All that pale skin and a bikini with your tits barely held in there."

To my surprise, Jorie's cheeks turn a little pink, but she fearlessly asks, "What else?"

"I wondered what your pussy tasted like." Her cheeks deepen from pink to red. "Then I went and took a shower and jacked off thinking about it."

"How old was I?" she whispers.

"Fifteen," I admit with a small pang of guilt hitting me in the middle of my chest. "But not again after what happened in that hotel suite that night."

She nods, her eyes going super soft with what I'd call hero worship. I know she thinks I saved her, but all I did was get her to the hospital.

And exact revenge.

"Want to know the first time I crushed on you?" she asks me mischievously.

"Does it involve details of you masturbating to thoughts of me?" I ask wickedly.

"Eww," she says while wrinkling her nose. "I said crush, not masturbate. I was ten."

My brows furrow as I try to think back that far. "What happened when you were ten?"

"I know you probably don't remember it," Jorie says

as she goes to her side to face me in the bed. Curling her arm under a pillow, she says, "Your parents were out of town and you threw a party. And I snuck over to watch through the living room window. My dad was out of town on a business trip and the nanny was sound asleep."

A niggling memory starts to surface, but I don't try to dig for it, preferring to let Jorie tell me the story.

"And a group of people were outside smoking a joint—a few guys and girls—and they found me there. They started messing around with me, offering me a hit. I got scared and decided to go back home, but one of the girls grabbed my wrist and tried to push the joint in my face."

I remember it as clear as day now, continuing with the memory. "And I came out, saw it, and went apeshit."

She nods with a smile. "I've never seen you so mad. You were cursing and yelling at them, and the entire time, you held my hand in yours. Ran them right off your property."

Man, was I pissed. Especially because the girl trying to make Jorie take a hit off that joint was some chick I'd been fucking. Can't even remember her name now.

"That was your first crush, huh?"

"My first, but not my last," she says impishly. "I moved on from you when Tony Greco pushed Sean Harp down on the playground when he tried to lift my dress up."

I bring my hand to my chest. "I'm wounded."

Giggling, Jorie wiggles a little closer to me and puts her hand on my hip where she strokes it lightly. "I was a little older when I started my dirty thoughts."

"I'm not sure we'll make it to breakfast if you tell me about it," I warn her. "But lay it on me."

"No way," Jorie says as she pops up to an elbow. Can't help it… my eyes go to her tits as they jiggle a little bit. Her nipples are redder than normal, and there's a bite mark on the side of her breast just below her scar. The tantalizing sight is impeded as she snaps her fingers in front of my eyes, and I blink. "Eyes up here, buddy."

I grin at her as I do as she asks.

"I'm hungry. Feed me."

"Fine," I say with a last, lingering look at her breasts. "But don't get dressed. You're not leaving after."

Her beaming smile at me isn't filled with just happiness over my demand, but also triumph. She knew before I did she wasn't leaving today.

CHAPTER 10

Jorie

TURNS OUT, WE both got dressed, but not after an honest attempt at naked breakfast.

It started off on the wrong foot because I felt too awkward with my ass sitting on a cold, leather bar stool at his kitchen island and my arms crossed over my chest. Walsh shot me an exasperated look as he pulled the eggs out of the fridge.

"Drop your hands, Jorie," he commanded. "You ingeniously argued your way into my bed so you're not about to deprive me of staring at your body."

I blushed and dropped my hands, the coolness from the air conditioning hardening my nipples.

Because I apparently couldn't look him in the eye in the bright light of day while he scrambled eggs, I stared at his cock, fascinated by it. He's way larger than Vince... than anyone I've ever been with, but that's a grand total of three men. The guy I lost my virginity to, which was a drunk hookup in college, Vince, and then

Walsh.

He had absolutely no shame as he moved with casual ease around his kitchen. His hair was pulled back again at the top, the length just brushing his shoulders. Walsh made a gorgeous picture, but I mostly just stared at his dick.

To my surprise, it started to move and lengthen.

My eyes flew up to his, and he was staring at me staring at him.

"Go put your clothes on," he said drily. "And bring me a pair of briefs out of my top dresser drawer. At this rate, both of us will perish from starvation."

I scurried to the bedroom and did as he asked, relieved not to have to feel awkward around Walsh. I expect we could move toward naked breakfast, but things are still too new on the sexual-discovery scale. You'd think after all the things Walsh has done to me, I'd be a bit freer with my body, but if anything, I might be more insecure. I guess I might feel inadequate after seeing up close and personal—repeatedly—how confident he is sexually. I'm not sure I measure up.

This thought sucks because this all leads back to Vince making me feel this way, and it's something I just don't like.

But now I've got on my panties and one of Walsh's t-shirts, which he told me was way sexier than me being naked anyway, and he has on a pair of very well-fitting boxer briefs in black. I make myself not look at the front, which has his beautiful package clearly outlined as he butters some toast.

I quietly watch him work, thinking I've never seen anything as inherently sexy as a man who feels confident in the kitchen.

In his underwear.

"What are we going to do today?" I ask him casually, and then I wince because that sounds so clingy. It also sounds bossy and intrusive, and much the way I imagined he viewed me when I was a little girl always demanding his and Micah's attention.

Walsh glances up at me, swallows his food, and smirks. "Some of us have jobs, Jorie. I have to go into the office."

Oh, shit. It's Monday. Given the fact I'm unemployed, and haven't worried about what day of the week it was for several now, it slipped my mind.

I glance over at the digital clock on the microwave. "But it's almost eleven."

Another smirk. "One of the perks of owning your own business. Besides, I texted my secretary early this morning to cancel any appointments I had before noon."

"Oh," I say and focus on my eggs. Pretty soon, I'll need to leave his place. Pretty soon, I'll know for sure whether Walsh will let me back in here. Last night, I goaded him into reacting to me, but I can't do that again. Not because I'm not that devious, because I am, but because I really don't want to go to The Wicked

Horse by myself. I don't think he'll call my bluff a second time.

"What are you going to do, Jor?" Walsh asks as he picks up his coffee to take a sip.

I shrug. "Oh, I don't know. I guess get some laundry done, maybe—"

"No," he interrupts. "What are you going to do with your life? You can't just hide out in Elena's apartment forever."

"I'm not hiding," I say hotly.

"Have you looked for a new job? Have you decided to stay in Henderson permanently? Or maybe move to San Francisco to be near Micah?"

"I don't know," I say in my surliest voice. "I haven't given it much thought."

"Why not?" he asks curiously. "You're a go-getter, Jorie. Always have been."

"Well, I'm sorry, Walsh," I snap. "I got kicked out of my own house three weeks ago because I was a lousy lay to my husband. I think I've been reeling a little bit and not sure what to do."

Walsh's eyes harden, and he sets his cup down. Leaning across the island, he says, "You are not a lousy lay. Stop thinking of yourself that way."

"I can't even have naked breakfast with you," I mutter. "I'm pretty sure I'm not good at this stuff."

"Hey," he says, and my eyes lock to his. "These last two nights, I've never come harder in my life. You drained me dry, Jorie, and trust me when I say… you're a fantastic fuck. Your husband is a moron."

I give him a weak smile and take a bite of my eggs.

Thankfully, he moves on from the topic of sex, but not thankfully, he moves back to prodding me about my life. "I'm assuming you quit your job when you came here?"

"Well, yeah. It was back in Los Angeles. I'm here in Nevada."

"Your job could be done from anywhere," Walsh points out, and I blink at him in surprise.

Then my lips curve upward. "You knew what my job was?"

Walsh shrugs. "Micah kept me a little up to date with what was going on with you."

I suppress my grin, because although we've lost touch for several years, Walsh knew I worked as a copyeditor—which was the most boring job ever and I hated it—but technically… I could do my job anywhere.

I graduated UCLA with a degree in journalism. I'd had starry-eyed visions of working for The Washington Post or reporting from war-ravaged countries, maybe even anchoring the CNN weekend news desk, but never in my wildest dreams did I think I'd be doing copyediting for a fashion magazine. It was long, awful hours of tedious work on subject matter I abhorred. One thing I was not sad to leave behind was that job.

"I'm rethinking my career path," is all I tell Walsh.

"Vince set me up a generous bank account so money is not an immediate concern right now."

He studies me a moment, perhaps hearing the failure in my voice, and he leaves it alone.

"What about your marriage?" he asks.

"What about it?" I ask vaguely.

"Well, you're married. Are you going to try to make it work?"

My eyebrows shoot high. "Excuse me? Why would I try to make it work?"

"Because you have years invested in it," Walsh says in a matter-of-fact tone. "What your husband did to you was awful but maybe not unforgivable."

I consider this for only a moment. "Did Micah tell you why I got married?"

Walsh goes still, a forkful of eggs dropping back to the plate as he slowly shakes his head.

"I was pregnant."

Walsh's eyes harden. "Micah never told me," he says.

"I'd dated Vince through most of my college years. He was five years older than me, and I found out I was pregnant just a month after graduating. Vince offered marriage, and I accepted."

Walsh straightens and pushes his plate away, his eggs half-eaten, his toast ignored. "What happened?"

I shrug and push my food around my plate, not overly hungry because this conversation turned heavy. "I miscarried before we got married, but we went ahead and did it anyway. I mean… we loved each other, so why not? My point being, we didn't necessarily get married because we felt we would spend the rest of our lives together."

"If you love each other, you should talk things out," Walsh says, but his voice is tight. I wonder if he's saying that because he believes in the sanctity of marriage or he just wants to push me away.

I'm not ready to accept either of those right now, so I turn the tables. "What about your marriage?"

I expect this to put Walsh on guard and maybe turn him defensive, but he acts all casual now as he leans back over the counter and grabs his fork. "What about it?"

He takes a bite, chews as if this is the easiest thing in the world to have a conversation about, and watches me… waits for me to ask more.

"Why did you get divorced?" I ask, not sure I want to know about how he got to the marriage part.

"We didn't have a lot of compatibility to make it long term," he tells me.

"But you had some compatibility," I push.

"Well, yeah, Jorie," he says with a smirk. "I didn't just marry some woman off the street."

"Did you love her?"

"Yes."

Ugh… why does that bother me?

"How were you incompatible? You're pushing me to work things out with Vince, so why didn't you work things out in your marriage?"

Walsh swallows some eggs he'd forked into his mouth, takes a napkin, and wipes his mouth while he appraises me, as if he's trying to figure out if I really want to know the truth to the questions I just asked.

Finally, he says, "The only thing we really had in common was sex. It was…"

He trails off as if trying to find the right word, so I supply it for him. "Good?"

"Fantastic," he corrects, and that makes my stomach sink. "It was so incredible for both of us, we thought it meant more than it did. In the end, it was just great sex. That wasn't enough to overcome all the other areas where we just weren't aligned."

"Like what?" I can't help but ask, because I want to compare her to myself.

"We had sex without a condom," Walsh says in return.

"Well, yeah… you were married. Why would that be an incompatibility?"

Walsh shakes his head, his eyes focusing hard on me. "*You and I* had sex without a condom. Half an hour ago. I didn't ask your permission, and you didn't protest."

"That's true," I say hesitantly, because he's veered so far off course from talking about his marriage that I'm having a tough time keeping up. Also, just thinking about the way he felt inside of me as he came, and the way he leaked out of me after…

I shake my head to get out of my head.

"Jorie… we had unprotected sex, and you don't seem to care."

"I'm on the pill," I tell him, even though he already knows since he did ask me about it just before thrusting inside of me.

Walsh rolls his eyes at me and growls, "Aren't you worried about STDs?"

My eyebrows knit in confusion. "No, why should I?"

"Jorie," Walsh says in exasperation. "Safe sex. STDs. How can you not be worried?"

Then it hits me. Walsh really doesn't understand that even though we haven't seen each other in years, it doesn't mean I don't know his core being.

"You'd never hurt me," I tell him simply. "You would have never taken it upon yourself to expose me to something like that. I figure if you took me without protection, you did so because you were clean. So, no… I wasn't worried then and I'm not worried now."

I expect this reasoning to make Walsh happy, but his jaw tightens. I'm insightful enough to know that he doesn't want me believing in him so much, because while he may never expose me to physical harm, I'm sure he's worried about the emotional wreckage someone like him could leave behind.

With a curt nod to my plate, Walsh says, "Finish up. I'm going to get a shower, and then I can have my driver take you back to your car."

I'm silent as Walsh puts his plate in the sink and turns to his bedroom. I have a million things I want do, none of which I can.

I want to crawl naked into the shower with him, take him back into my mouth, and make him see me as something other than a little sister.

I want to pull him back to the counter and make him talk to me. I want to know more about his marriage, and why he is so opposed to relationships now. I want to know if we could ever be anything to each other than just sex.

But I can tell he's closed off for now, and I should back off. Walsh is a man who doesn't like to be pushed too far, and I'm a woman smart enough to know how to play this cool.

Still, I can't help but call out. "Walsh?"

He stops, turns slightly to look at me.

"Why weren't you worried about having unprotected sex with me? You didn't ask me if I was clean."

"Same as you," he says quietly. "I knew you'd never do something to hurt me. You were trying to push my bare cock into you, and you would have only done that if you were safe."

My heart soars with his admission that we're tight enough he trusted me on something that's important in a sexual relationship. I'm satisfied enough to let him walk off without any further conversation.

CHAPTER 11

Walsh

Taking a deep breath, I step up to the rack, squat, and position the bar over the back of my shoulders. It's loaded with three hundred and twenty-five pounds. Certainly not my personal best, but I'm not going for heavyweight, only repetitions.

I take another breath, push up against the weight to stand straight, then take two steps back from the rack. I exhale, inhale again, and squat. The breath pushes out of me hard as I stand back up.

I do this for a total of six reps and then manage to maneuver the barbell back onto the rack. I'm streaming sweat from every pore in my body, and my legs are shaking from that last set.

One of the perks of being incredibly wealthy is having all the toys. I'd outfitted my apartment with a world-class gym, and I take advantage of it every single day. If I'm not power-lifting, I'm running. I'm doing something every day because exercise is the second-best way for me to destress from my hectic life.

Sex obviously being the first one, but that situation's all fucked up, so I worked out extra hard tonight after I left the office.

Grabbing a towel and my water, I first mop my face, then drink the entire contents of the bottle. I toss it in the waste bin that my housekeeper will ensure gets to recycling, and head to my master bath for a shower.

Just as I'm entering my bedroom, I hear my phone vibrating on the nightstand where I'd left it with the ringer turned off and charging. As I walk closer, I see Micah's name on the screen.

I'd like to avoid him right now, but that will do nothing but feed my guilt, so I answer it reluctantly.

"What's up, man?" I say casually as if the weight of his little sister weren't resting on my shoulders.

"Not much," he says. "Just checking in with you. Did Jorie get up with you?"

"What?" I ask, freaked his first question would be about his sister.

"She texted me yesterday morning for your phone number," Micah says casually, apparently not picking up on my distress, thank fuck. "Said she was in Vegas and was going to try to get up with you for lunch."

Fuck. Is he testing me? Did Jorie tell him we talked? Had lunch? Do I lie? Do I tell him the truth that we did, in fact, hookup but not for lunch. We hooked up and fucked all night.

Goddamn it.

"Um… no," I say, throwing caution to the wind and lying my ass off. "She didn't."

I wince and wait for Micah's next words, my entire frame feeling weak with the guilt for what I'm doing. I'm not always a good guy, but I am loyal and forthright with my friends. Especially Micah.

Always with Micah, actually.

Until I fucked Jorie.

Shit. Shit. Shit.

"Well, you might want to give her a call," Micah suggests, and I exhale so hard in relief my lungs almost completely deflate. "I think she's been a little down since all this shit with Vince. It would be nice for her to see a friendly face."

Like friendly as in my face between her legs? Because she's seen that plenty.

"Yeah, sure thing, buddy," I say as I walk into my bathroom, then move to change the subject. "What's up with you?"

"Aren't you going to ask for her number?" Micah asks.

More guilt… a punch to the gut that I'm doing something Micah would go ballistic and would probably sever our friendship over. "I'm getting ready to jump in the shower and don't have anything to write it down with. Just text it to me," I say easily.

"Will do," he returns. "So, I'm working on an updated design for a power dildo."

I laugh, relieved to be talking about dildos with my best friend. "What's the concept?" I ask as I turn on the shower and step back to let the water warm up. I lean against the marbled vanity as I listen to Micah explain.

The man is a brilliant engineer and founded a premier firm in San Francisco almost five years ago. He'd started out in Michigan after graduating from college, soaked up as much knowledge on the business side as he could, and moved to northern California after Jorie turned of age.

But despite his success and money, he's turned a kinky hobby into a business concept that might have some legs. He started dabbling in these sex machines just to get his girlfriends' rocks off, but Jerico paid him good money for that dildo machine and the chance to try it out, and a niche business suddenly looks to be feasible. Micah can certainly do it on the side and still maintain his professional business.

"What do you think?" he asks me solemnly after he tells me about the concept.

Let's see... he envisions a contraption that will hoist a spread-eagled, tied-with-rope woman in the air and drill a mechanical power dildo into her from above?

"Fucking fantastic idea," I tell him, and my dick gets rock hard as an image of Jorie in that contraption erupts within my mind.

Christ. My hand goes to rub myself through my gym

shorts, but then my erection starts to fade when Micah says, "Thought you'd like that. But listen… I got to go. I'm texting you Jorie's number. Maybe take her out to lunch or breakfast or something, okay? Help get her mind off that asshole husband of hers."

"Okay," I say hoarsely as a wave of shame from my deception threatens to render me impotent forever.

That's it. Decision made. I absolutely cannot do this with Jorie.

"Thanks, man," he says. "You're the best."

"Back at you," I mutter, and we say our goodbyes.

I turn and set my phone on the vanity, the shower now emitting steam from behind me. Morose eyes stare back at me from the mirror. There's a woman I want more than anything in the world, and I absolutely cannot have her.

Micah made sure of that three years ago after my divorce finalized with Renee.

It was a time to get together with my best friend and confidant. To mourn the loss of my marriage, or perhaps it was to celebrate since it started a new chapter in my life. Micah never came to Vegas because he hated the glitz and touristy nature. He had no family left at all except for Jorie, and she was in Los Angeles living her life. I often chartered a plane to San Francisco to party with Micah, so it was the logical place for me to go the weekend after I got the divorce papers filed.

We got drunk.

Well, I got supremely drunk that first night.

Shit faced.

I woke up in his apartment, in the guest bedroom with a naked woman on top of me. I remember raising my throbbing head off the pillow and looking at her with bleary eyes, not recognizing her or remembering a damn thing about what we did.

After I rolled her off me, I stumbled into Micah's kitchen, jonesing for some coffee and promising myself I'd never drink again. My stomach was threatening to rebel. My headache was so intense everything was blurry.

I found Micah in the kitchen, wearing nothing but a pair of boxer shorts, sipping at his coffee. He didn't greet me, but I didn't notice at the time, or think anything was off.

After pouring my coffee, I sat across the table and muttered, "Sorry about the woman in there. Hope we weren't too loud."

Micah put his cup down. "We brought her home together."

Despite the pain in my head, my eyebrows raise in interest. We'd shared women before, but it had been a long time. "I don't remember. What did I miss?"

"The usual," he said, which meant one of us had her pussy and the other had her ass at the same time.

"Let me get my stomach and head settled, and we can give her a nice send-off," I told him with a grin, then winced at the pain that caused.

"You really don't remember?" Micah asked, and that's

when I noted something funny in his voice.

I didn't shake my head in denial because it would have hurt too much, but I told him the truth. "Completely blacked out. How much did I drink last night?"

"Enough to make you black out, apparently," he said with heat to his voice.

"Did I do something to piss you off?" I asked flatly.

Micah's eyes narrowed. "Does my sister Jorie ring a bell?"

I honestly had no clue what he was talking about. Jorie had been living in Los Angeles for several years. I hadn't seen her in forever, and didn't know much of what was going on other than she was married to some financial advisor or some shit like that.

"Jorie?" I asked in confusion.

"You don't remember the shit you told me last night?" he asked with disbelief.

Dread welled up inside of me, because that could only mean a couple of things. I either professed my attraction to his sister, or I spilled the beans about what happened to her when she was sixteen, a secret Jorie and I had kept solidly together.

"Why don't you enlighten me?" I asked, but I sure as hell didn't want to know the answer.

"After we fucked that woman in there," he said with a jerk of his head toward the hallway that led to the bedrooms, "we came out to the living room and drank some more. You were bitching and moaning about Renee."

"Bitching and moaning?" This was odd because Renee and I mutually decided to end the marriage. There was nothing really to bitch or moan about, except for the fact I was going to miss having sex with her.

"About how you shouldn't have bothered with marrying her."

I could totally see me saying that because it was the truth. I was smart enough to have a prenup signed with Renee, but she still left the marriage with a nice chunk of my money. Still, I didn't begrudge it to her. I knew what I was getting into.

"What does that have to do with Jorie?" I asked.

"You started talking weird shit about Jorie," Micah said. "It made no sense."

"Like what?" I prodded, my stomach tightening, the one sip of coffee I'd had threatening to come up.

"That you didn't have a special bond with Renee, not the way you did with Jorie," he said, and bile rose in my throat. "I asked you what that meant, but you just kept repeating that, all slurred and not making sense."

"Okay," I said hesitantly.

"Until you appeared to sober up miraculously for just a moment," Micah said through gritted teeth. "You looked at me and said, 'If you could have just seen the way she looked at me, brother... I've never had anyone look at me like that before.'"

I wanted to mutter every curse word in the dictionary, because while I had no recollection about what I'd said while drunk, I knew exactly what I was referencing.

I was talking about the moment I walked into that bathroom in that hotel suite to rescue Jorie. When I walked in that door, the utter look of worship in her eyes almost made me stumble. Like I was her hero, or that if she never saw another thing as long as she lived, she'd be satisfied with that one moment where I came to save her.

"Did you fuck my sister?" Micah growled.

"What?" I barked back at him, stunned he would even think that. He actually jerked his head back at my tone. "Fuck, no. Why would you ever ask me something like that?"

"What did you expect me to think?" he retorted, but the heat had died from his voice. "What did you mean 'the way she looked at you'?"

This was dicey. I couldn't share Jorie's secret.

I lied for the first time about Jorie to my best friend who was like my brother. "I don't know, Micah. Maybe I was talking about how when we were growing up together, and Jorie would fucking follow us around all the time. She looked up to us, man. We were her heroes, dude. Surely you remember that?"

I hated turning the tables on him like that, but I had to deflect the pressure off me. Micah's eyes softened as he admitted, "Yeah… that little monster wouldn't leave us alone."

"She was a little monster, wasn't she?" I chuckled with relief. "Look… you know I love Jorie like a sister. I have no

clue why she came into the conversation about Renee last night, but maybe I just wanted that from my marriage. To be her hero or something."

God those words tasted like shit on my tongue. Not only from the lie inside of them but because I never in my life wanted to be that to a woman. I'd been that to Jorie for just a few hours of my life and the connection was so intense, it was almost painful. Letting her go completely from that type of emotional connection sucked hairy balls, and I sure as shit didn't want Renee looking like that at me. It smacked too much of an emotional commitment I wasn't ready to give, even to my wife.

"Alright, dude," Micah said with a nervous laugh. "I get it. But fuck... the thought of you and Jorie together. Christ, it gave me the willies. Talk about fucking wrong, Walsh."

"So wrong," I'd agreed with him because I was on the same wavelength. She was like a little sister to me, but more importantly, she had moved on.

At that time, it wasn't a lie when I told him, "You have no worries, bro. Jorie's too much like a sister to me to ever even consider that."

And that is the real reason I can't be with Jorie. That's the reason why I know without a doubt Micah would never accept me fucking his little sister. He told me it was wrong, and I fucking agreed with him. He's got every right to expect me to keep my distance.

I look down to my phone and think about the texts

Jorie had sent me this afternoon. When I packed her off this morning, I evaded making plans with her by telling her I might have to work late. I hadn't responded to her two texts asking me if I was, in fact, working late.

She wanted to come over, and God save my soul, I wanted her to.

But I couldn't let her.

I pick up my phone and respond to her last message with a simple, *Sorry. Caught up in late meetings and still working. Can't see you tonight.*

It was lame and it was a lie, but I've gotten good at those over the last few days apparently. I set the phone back down and turn to the shower. I'm going to get cleaned up and then head to The Wicked Horse to finish putting Jorie out of my mind.

CHAPTER 12

Jorie

"WELL, LOOK WHAT the cat dragged in," I say with a smile as Elena walks into her apartment. She immediately flops down in her favorite living room chair, a big cushy thing done in pink and green paisley that makes my eyes hurt.

Pushing off her tennis shoes, she puts her feet up on the matching ottoman with a groan. "Remind me why I work seven days a week?"

Normally, Elena has Sunday and Monday off from the hair salon where she works, Saturday, of course, being her busiest day of the week. But she's on a mission to buy her first house because as she said, "I need to be more adult-like before I hit thirty."

As such, she works eighty-hour weeks and squirrels her money away.

"Want something to eat?" I ask as I set my Kindle aside. I'd been relaxing today, just as I have every day since I've moved here. It's nice not having a job, but I can't live off Vince forever.

"What I want," Elena says dramatically, "is to know how many orgasms you had last night?"

The only thing she knows is that I was with Walsh because I had texted her such and not to expect me home.

I can't help but smile at her as I put my feet up on the coffee table. Pulling a pink satin pillow with tassels onto my lap, I hug it to my chest and ask her, "What do you want to know?"

"How many fucking orgasms?" she reiterates.

Chuckling, I tell her, "Too many to count."

"What rooms did you use at the club?" She pulls her legs from the ottoman and crosses them under her, leaning forward so as not to miss details.

"We didn't stay at the club." I recount with a fond smile how I goaded Walsh into having sex with me. "I told him I was going to have sex with some other guy or I could have sex with him, and he pulled me out of the club, threw me in his car, and took me to his apartment."

"Would you have really had sex with someone else?" she asks. In my opinion, it's an absolutely unimportant question because she knows me better.

"No way," I tell her staunchly. "It was a bluff and he didn't call it last night."

"So, back to orgasms," she prods.

"He's amazing," I tell her with a smile on my face.

"The sex... God, Elena... it's like nothing I ever imagined. When we first got to his apartment, he put me on my knees and then…"

I hesitate because it's almost too dirty to say. But she merely cocks an eyebrow at me that says, *"Girl… you rode a power dildo for that man… nothing could be dirtier than that."*

That's true.

"He fucked my face," I tell her.

Her eyes get round, and she leans forward so far, I'm afraid she'll topple to the ottoman. "Damn, that's so hot. Did you deep throat him?"

I shake my head with a grin. "No. My gag reflex sucks, but he started trying to overcome it later."

"How?"

"He was… um… fucking me on my back, and he put his finger in my mouth and told me to suck it. And so, I did. Then he pushed it back further a little each time, until he had me swallowing it. I was so discombobulated by him hammering me into the mattress, I didn't even think about my gag reflex."

"My panties are wet," Elena says as she grins at me. "Seriously wet. Vince would shit his pants if he knew about this. I want to email him right now."

"Knew about what?" I ask her curiously.

Vince didn't expect me to be celibate because he'd emailed me two days after I'd returned to Henderson to tell me that he thought it was best we have the freedom to "explore other options". That translated to him wanting to have sex with other women, and it crushed me. I cried for two straight days after that and wouldn't come out of my room.

"Isn't it clear?" Elena asks.

"Apparently not," I say dryly.

"Vince was the one who was bad at sex," Elena says. "I know you haven't told me about every sexual thing you've done with him, but I'm pretty sure the most exciting thing you two did was he had you give him a hand job in an empty movie theater. Woo-hoo. That just screams never-ending orgasms."

I laugh at my friend, not because she's silly—because she totally is—but because she can freely admit her dislike of Vince now. I mean, I always knew she didn't like him but she was a good friend. She tolerated him because I loved him.

When we decided to get married because of the baby, Elena voiced her opinion to me once, and that was to tell me that she didn't think that was a good reason to get married. But she didn't harass me about it; she let me make my own choices.

Not long after we married, Vince told me one night that he had been scared shitless about the prospect of parenthood. He went on to tell me he wasn't ready, and maybe the miscarriage was God's way of telling us to slow down. I essentially took that to mean that Vince didn't really want kids. Elena was there to listen to me cry heartbroken through the phone. She didn't even tell me "I told you so" once even though she had reason to.

But I stuck with that damn marriage because I thought love could triumph and that as Vince got older, he'd get the desire for kids one day.

Sadly, that never manifested. Maybe that's why things broke down between us. I wanted kids like I wanted to see a sunrise every morning. Maybe I stopped being good enough in bed because sex with him was just sex and nothing else. It wasn't a means to create something more beautiful.

My phone rings on the couch beside me and I grab it, holding it up and hoping to see Walsh's name. He's not responded to my texts today, but I also know he was working.

"Oh, shit," I say as my eyes pop up to Elena as I take in the name on my screen. "It's Vince."

"Jesus," she mutters. "It's like he knew I was telling you he was a shitty lover."

Snickering, I shoot her an amused wink and answer the phone. It's the first time we've talked since I left the house. "Hello."

"Hey, Jorie," he says, and I recognize that tone in his voice. It's conciliatory. He wants something.

"What do you want, Vince?" I ask in a tired voice. Just with two words—Hey, Jorie—he tired me out.

"I want to check in on you," he says softly but with a tiny hint of offense.

"Why?" I ask in confusion.

He's silent a moment before he says, "Because I miss you."

"Oh, hell no," I snap into the phone, and Elena's eyes go wide. "You do not get to do that."

Normally, if I were to talk to him in the way I just did—all combative and itching to fight—he would come at me with barrels blazing.

Instead, he sets me on my heels by quietly stating, "It's true. I've been really thinking things over, and I think I made a mistake."

"Figured out maybe I was a better lay than the other women you've been out fucking?" I ask acidly.

Another moment of silence before he says, "I've been with a few women, Jorie. But this is something else. I miss *you*. My wife. I miss you in bed and at my kitchen table and in my car when we drive up the coast. I miss talking to you after an exhausting day of work when we're eating macaroni and cheese out of the box, and well… everything. Eight years of memories we've built up, and I destroyed them in a fit of middle-aged distress."

"You're not even middle-aged, Vince," I say but the sarcasm in my head doesn't come through in my voice. That's clearly because he's shocked me by his candid words and earnest demeanor.

"Maybe I'm just old enough to realize that what I thought was important wasn't and what is important I didn't realize until you left."

"Huh?" Totally confused.

"Jorie… I want you to come home," he says. "I'll go to counseling if you want. We can talk things through. We can get you a sex therapist or something—"

"What the fuck, Vince?" I practically screech into the phone. "You can't say something that demeaning to me and think I'm going to run back into your arms."

"What?" he asks, completely clueless. "I'm just trying to be honest with you."

My insides boil with rage, and I'm dizzy from what I think might be an unnatural rise in my blood pressure. When I cut my eyes to Elena, she looks back at me with her head tilted and her expression worried.

I take a deep breath and let my nasty bitch come out. "There's nothing wrong with the way I have sex, Vince. See… I've been doing a little exploring myself."

I hear his sharp intake of breath because I can tell he never thought I had something like that in me. Well, guess what, Vince? You don't know the gumption deep inside the woman you married and then broke her heart.

"Just last night, I dropped to my knees as soon as we hit his apartment and I let him fuck my face so hard, I cried. Then he ate me out and gave me three orgasms in a row. I'm sorry things aren't going so well for you, but they are fucking fantastic on my end."

I wait with glowing self-satisfaction for him to say something in return, but I get nothing but silence.

Dead silence.

"Vince?" I say tentatively into the phone.

Nothing.

I look back to Elena. "He hung up on me."

"Holy shit, I can't believe you told him about last night. You're evil and genius and I want to marry you. Divorce Vince and marry me."

I give a tiny chuckle, but I'm immediately flooded with guilt that I said those things. I know they had to hurt, and I've never been one to strike out so viciously just to assuage my own hurt.

"I should call him back," I say with a heavy, guilt-laden voice.

"You should do no such thing." Elena's voice is harsh. "He deserved every word of that. He put you down and made you doubt yourself. Your words didn't throw his deficiencies at him but rather pointed out that you're worthy. There was nothing wrong with you doing that."

Is she right?

Did he deserve that?

And did I deserve to have guilt-free sex with Walsh? Was I using him to put a bandage on my battered self-esteem?

Speaking of Walsh, I flip to my texts and frown when I see he's sent me a response. *Sorry. Caught up in late meetings and still working. Can't see you tonight.*

"Asshole," I mutter under my breath.

"What?" Elena asks cautiously.

"Walsh just blew me off," I tell her as I toss the phone her way. She catches it, turns it to face her, and reads his texts.

"I don't get it," she says in puzzlement, tossing my phone back to me.

"I don't either," I tell her as I stand up resolutely. "He's definitely past thinking of me as a little sister, so the hang up has to be with Micah."

"Why would Micah care if you and Walsh were together?" she asks.

I shrug as I head toward my bedroom to pull together a sexy outfit. "I have no clue, but I'm going to find out."

"Are you going to his apartment?"

"Yup," I call over my shoulder. "And I'm not leaving until he sees me. I hope Bentley is a good conversationalist."

CHAPTER 13

Walsh

I SIT AT the bar in The Silo, sipping at a vodka on the rocks. The rocks are all melted and its mostly watered vodka but I take my time with it. I've violated my "no alcohol when fucking at the club" rule again, but I'm not going to let it stop me from what I came here to do.

Prove to myself that Jorie doesn't matter to me.

I've put off a few women who have approached me. I've watched some of the fucking going on, and I'm horny as hell as evidenced by the semi I've been sporting for the last hour. But nothing's caught my interest enough to leave this barstool.

Even watching what's going on inside the room with Micah's dildo contraption isn't enticing me. It's rare that Jerico and his girlfriend, Trista, come in to play. He never shares her physically with another man, but he doesn't mind people watching what he does to her.

She doesn't mind either, for that matter, because she only ever has eyes for Jerico. I've been watching them for a few minutes in that room as he kissed her slowly and teased the crowd with a slow removal of her clothes. He put her up against the glass, stood behind her while he fingered her to orgasm, and then had her suck his fingers clean.

Then he put her on the machine and I was instantly turned on. I watched as he used the remote control to get her close to another orgasm, and then slow it down just to torture her. When she was begging, he powered it up hard and fast, and she screamed so loud I could hear her clearly through the glass.

Fuck, I wanted Jorie back in there and ten minutes with that machine. The things I could do…

"Christ," I mutter and pick up my watered vodka to take a sip.

My eyes scan the room, hoping against hope I find someone who attracts me.

As fate would have it, my cock goes from half hard to concrete as I watch with disbelief as Jorie walks into the room. She's wearing the same dress she had on two nights ago when I fucked her in here. She looks to the room where Jerico is now fucking Trista doggie style, but she doesn't watch. Her eyes scan the rest of the rooms, and I see her shoulders relax in relief.

She's here looking for me, or rather… looking to see if I'm with someone else.

With a half turn, she sees me at the bar and narrows her eyes at me with purpose as she starts walking my way.

I slam down the rest of my drink as I pay attention to the way she's strutting. Hips swaying, breasts ready to spill out of that stretchy fabric.

I also don't fail to notice other men looking at her and a wave of protectiveness overcomes me. And it's not in a brotherly way, but in one that makes me want to throw her down on the floor, fuck her, and spray my load all over her tits to mark her.

"Christ," I mutter again as she reaches me.

"Late night working, huh?" she asks with a plastered smile on her face, but there's enough hurt in her voice that it makes me feel like shit.

"Got done earlier than I thought," I tell her blandly.

"And you thought to come here?"

"It was one of a few thoughts," I admit to her. "It turns out once I thought hard enough about it, it was really my only option."

Jorie steps in closer, and her scent assaults me. I try not to focus on that bright red lipstick and how good it would feel to have her smear it on my cock again.

"Walsh… why can't I be an option?" she asks softly but with so much desperation in her voice I want to fucking kick my own ass for touching her.

"Doesn't matter," I tell her, not willing to engage because she might argue me right into having sex with her again. The wench should have gone to law school rather than get a journalism degree. "Just know it's over."

A predatory gleam enters Jorie's eyes, and a thrill of

fear races through me as I have no recognition of this sexual creature who moves in closer to me again. Her hand comes to my stomach, and she goes on tiptoes to put her lips closer to my ear so she can whisper, "It's not over, Walsh. I've been wet for you all day. If you doubt me, you can just put your hand between my legs to find out. I'm not wearing any panties."

My fingers itch to touch her and my dick is throbbing painfully. Jorie was always a confident kid growing up. She was the leader of her group of friends. She was an extrovert and didn't have a shy bone in her body. But this woman standing before me having the utmost faith in herself has me reeling. If she was talking dirty like this to Vince, and showed the same confidence to him, I can't for the life of me figure out how sex was bad between them.

Of course, he's probably got a little pecker and doesn't even know how to make Jorie come.

"I can't give you what a woman like you should have," I tell her in an attempt to let her down easily. "You know this about me. I don't do relationships. It's just fucking."

"And I think I told you that I'm okay with that," she says as she leans back slightly to look me in the eye.

Shaking my head, I try to reason with her, "You don't want to do this, Jorie. Trust me. This lifestyle of casual sex isn't good for a girl like you."

"Woman," she clarifies.

I nod. "Woman. A woman who is sweet and sensitive and caring. You need someone who shares intimacy with you, not just impersonal fucking."

"It could be you," she suggests softly.

"It can't," I tell her bluntly. "It would only be sex with me."

"And again… I'm fine with that," she throws back at me.

"Christ, you're driving me crazy," I say with complete exasperation.

Jorie drops her hand and takes a step backward, her eyes cooling and her voice sounding all businesslike. "Look, Walsh… it's really very simple. I like sex. My husband thought I was bad at it, and I suspect I just didn't push myself hard enough. I'm going to figure it out, though. I'm going to figure it out now, and I'm not waiting for my next Prince Charming to sweep me off my feet. I'm not asking you for more. Why can't you get that I'm okay with that?"

What a mouthful and I hated hearing every word of it because she's telling me it's okay to have her in the only way I know how. Hated it so much, I should have just shoved my cock down her throat to shut her up.

But that's not going to happen, so I finally opt for the truth in the hopes that my transparency will at least get her to take me seriously. "I can't do this with you because of Micah."

Her beautiful, jet-black eyebrows pull inward. "What

do you mean 'because of Micah'? He has nothing to do with who I choose to fuck. I thought we'd already been through that. It hasn't stopped you yet."

"No," I admit "But he wouldn't approve of us, and that's why we can't keep going on."

"You can't possibly know that," she says in exasperation.

"I can," I tell her adamantly. "Because we've had the conversation, and he made it clear you are off limits to me."

"That's ridiculous," she sputters. "He has no say over what I do."

This is true, but moot.

"He has no say over what *you* do," she continues.

Also true, but I ask, "You want me to risk my friendship with him? Because if he found out, it would harm it irrevocably, and you're just going to have to trust me on that."

Jorie pulls her bottom lip between her teeth to worry at it, and when it pops free, she steps back into me. Both hands come to my chest, slide up, and hook over my shoulders. Her face comes close to mine and her voice is husky. "You and I kept a secret from Micah before. About that night and what happened. I propose we keep another secret."

"Lie to him about us?" I ask her with distaste, although truth be told, my interest is piqued. Well, my cock's interest is piqued… painfully so. My conscience isn't exactly on board.

"No, not lie. Just not tell him," she says. "I told you I'm okay with casual sex. Micah lives in San Francisco. We do our thing and don't make a big deal of it. Micah doesn't need to know, and I don't believe we have an obligation to tell him."

Everything about this is wrong, and yet the fact Jorie and I have kept a dark secret from Micah before gives me a bond with her that can't be ignored. I mean, if Micah had ever asked me point blank, "Walsh... has Jorie ever been nearly raped before and have you ever kept that from me?" I'd have to answer him truthfully.

But until that time, what he doesn't know doesn't hurt him.

Same concept here, right?

I must still look unconvinced because Jorie says, "Vince called me today. He wants me to come home."

My entire body goes rigid at the thought.

She continues, "You told me perhaps I should think about working it out."

I nod and hold my breath.

"But I can't," she says, and the air in my lungs comes out in a massive rush of relief. "I want to continue to figure out my sexuality, and Walsh... I want to do that with you. I want to do it in your apartment, in this club, and in the back of your limo. I want it everywhere."

I'm on edge, at risk of doing major violence if someone were to interrupt this conversation and so fucking horny, I'd probably come if Jorie laid her hand on my hard cock through my jeans. I clench my hands into fists, having no fucking clue what to do with this situation.

Jorie leans in, brushing her lips against mine before moving them to my jaw. They feel so soft as she slides them to my ear, and she whispers, "I'll let you do anything to me you want, Walsh. No limits. Whatever your dirtiest desire is."

She lets the implication drift away, and all of a sudden, all I can hear is the sounds of sex going on around us. I'd managed to tune it out for the last few hours. Grunts, moans, cries of climax, cries of pain, and slapping of flesh. It all filters in and an overwhelming need for Jorie sweeps through me.

Not desire.

Not passion.

Need.

My hands shoot out to grab her ass, pulling her all the way in between my legs as I slam my mouth down on hers. Her tiny cry of pleasure and surprise ramps me up, and I bring a hand down between her legs to indeed find her without panties and sopping wet.

The kiss is electric as my fingers play at the juncture of her legs. Jorie issues a tiny moan that I suck down into my throat as my tongue twirls against hers.

Fucking amazing. Jorie tastes sweeter and better than anything I've ever had in my mouth before. I've known this woman her entire life and yet she tastes like a deep dark mystery to me. A mystery I want to delve into and figure out. Untwist the shit inside her head and build her back up. I want to kiss her forever and…

I shoot off the stool, my need for Jorie making me crazed. I spin us around, bend her over the stool and push her skirt up over her hips. She spreads her legs for me obscenely and her pussy glistens from behind. I give it a light slap of my hand that leaves my palm wet. Jorie cries out, and I do it again.

"Walsh… please," she groans as I do it a third time.

Holy fuck, I need inside her.

My hands fumble at my belt, my button, and zipper. My cock hurts when I pull it out, and I don't waste a further second of time but thrust it deep inside of her from behind. A long groan of satisfaction, relief, and a sense of belonging rumbles out of my chest.

I pull back, seeing my wet cock briefly before I plunge it back in deeply.

Jorie urges me on, "Again."

My head spins with the need to come, but I need Jorie to get there first. I pull all the way out, my dick bobbing up and down in lost confusion. I slap her pussy again from behind a few times, then push through her lips with my finger to find her clit. I rub it hard, then slap her again. She shrieks every time I do it, each subsequent slap to those wet, puffy lips a little harder. I do this a few more times and when I pinch her clit, she screams out her release.

Fuck, that is the hottest thing.

She's still shaking as I drive back into her, my orgasm already starting to bubble down low in my groin. I look around, vaguely taking in the faces of some of the people watching with lust in their eyes. The bartender right on the other side of the bar watches from two feet away, and I can tell he's rubbing his dick.

But that all fades away as I fuck Jorie harder than I've ever fucked before. I make sure everyone in this club knows that, at least for now, this pussy is mine and only mine.

"I'm coming again," Jorie whimpers as she clamps down tight on me.

That's all I need. My head swims, my balls tighten, and I pull out of her just as I start unloading. I stroke my cock hard and fast, watching the white ropes of my semen splash all over her ass with a little bit getting on her dress.

I push back into her for a few more strokes, can feel more coming out of me as I groan out the rest of my release.

Jorie makes a sound of dismay when I pull out again, and because my dick is still hard for the moment, I rub it in my cum and then slide it through the cheeks of her ass.

That's next on my agenda... that ass.

But not right now.

Instead, I'm taking Jorie back to my apartment and

I'm going to do all the dirty things to her she said I could, but I'm going to do them slowly.

And privately.

CHAPTER 14

Jorie

MY BACK ARCHES and my hips shoot off the bed as I orgasm, and I'm so exhausted all I can manage is a groan of relief. I flop back down to the mattress, but Walsh doesn't stop. His tongue continues to move over me, in me... leaving no spot untouched or unworshipped.

"Please stop," I beg him as I push weakly at his head. He doesn't stop so I fist his hair and give it a hard tug.

He finally looks up at me with lazy eyes, his mouth wet and his smile satisfied.

"Enough," I tell him, then tug on his hair harder so he starts to climb up my body.

We've been going at it all night, into the early morning hours, and while I don't want to be done, I do want to catch my breath. Surely Walsh wants to catch his as he was just drowning in between my legs for what felt like hours.

Walsh comes up over me, elbows to the mattress and

his hips dipping down. I bring my arms up to circle around his neck, give him a hug and then a kiss to taste myself on his mouth, but he shocks me by sliding right inside of me.

He groans, closes his eyes, and rests his forehead on mine.

"I know I should stop," he mutters as he moves with lazy strokes. "But I can't."

Feeling the length of him inside of me, the press of him against my walls, and the sounds rumbling in his chest, I don't want him to quit either. I raise my legs, press my knees against his ribs, and move my hips counter to his.

I don't know how it's possible but, within minutes, he has me coming again. I gasp as my body trembles. Walsh continues to ride me slowly, lifting his face up so he can look at me.

"Helluva secret we've got going on here," he murmurs, stroking deep and true.

"And I'm okay with that," I tell him with a smile. I just hope to God Micah doesn't find out about this, not because I'm worried about my brother, but because it's important to Walsh. I want Walsh, but not at the expense of their friendship. Deep in my heart, I know this will only end in one way, and that's me eventually having to give him up.

But for right now, I'm selfish enough to take advantage of the deal we've struck.

Walsh's breathing gets heavier, his thrusts driving a little deeper. He's close. I've watched enough of him reaching his climax that I can recognize it clearly.

A few more thrusts and right there…

He plants deep, goes still, and groans with his eyes shut, muscles in his neck corded tight. The pleasure on his face the most erotic and beautiful thing I've ever seen, and it makes me wonder what I look like when I come. Based on some of the sounds I've made, I really don't want to see the corresponding facial expression.

Walsh rolls off me, goes to his side, and his fingers go back between my legs. Before I can even comprehend what he's doing, they're dipping inside of me, gathering his semen, then he's rubbing it in circles around my clit.

"Enough," I growl at him as my hand locks around his wrist. He's way stronger than I am so the only reason he stops is due to my command.

He grins at me and says, "One more orgasm."

"No," I huff out. "I'm exhausted."

Leaning over, I see his smile has softened before his lips press to mine. When he pulls back, I lose his lips and his fingers as he murmurs, "Fine. I'll give you a break."

"It's appreciated," I say in such a prissy voice Walsh barks out a laugh as I snuggle into his side.

Resting my head on his chest, I revel in the feel of his skin against mine and the way his arm wraps around me to stroke my hip.

My eyes start to droop, but I don't want to let this

incredible night come to an end yet. "Why didn't you come to my wedding?" I ask him softly.

His hand stills briefly but then resumes the soft strokes. "It's complicated."

"I'll help you figure it out," I tell him.

"Actually, *you're* complicated," he says like a true smartass, but then adds on, "I thought you were tired. Go to sleep."

"Tell me," I say as slide my arm over his stomach to hold him.

He's quiet a moment but finally says, "I jerked off to a fifteen-year-old girl that I looked at like a sister. I was fucking twenty-three. It doesn't get any more perverted than that."

"Oh, come on, Walsh," I chide as I raise my head to give him an admonishing look. "We all have fantasies."

"True," he says, and I can tell it's not the age difference or the dirty thoughts of a fifteen-year-old that's bothering him. "But that all changed after you were attacked."

"But why?" I ask in astonishment. "You were there for me. I know it made me feel closer to you."

"It made me realize you were just a young girl," he says firmly. "And far too innocent for me. I liked my sex raw and filthy, and even if you reached adulthood, I just couldn't dirty you up like that. I refused to do it, so I pulled you out of that compartment in my mind and put you firmly in the little sister room."

"Just like that?" I ask.

"Just like that," he says as his hand comes up to push my head back down onto his chest. "I never let myself have another fantasy about you. And I stayed away from your wedding because I didn't want to be tempted."

"Never thought of me like that again?" I whisper, more to myself than anything. That kind of hurts that I could be so easily forgotten.

"Not until I saw those scars on your breast the other night and realized I was inside of you," he says with a hint of bitterness in his voice. "I still don't get it."

"Get what?"

"How the fuck I didn't recognize your eyes." His voice is deep, pensive. This has bothered him, I can tell. "That shade of green that I've never seen on anyone else. How did I not see it was you?"

"Because you didn't want to," I offer him unsolicited advice. "If you really put me out of your mind, then you didn't want to see."

"This is so fucking complicated," he mutters. "I can't stand we're keeping this from Micah, and yet, I can't bear for him to know. I don't want to give this up, yet I know this isn't right for you."

"Stop trying to figure out what is right for me," I tell him as my head comes back off his chest. "I'm an adult woman who has got a pretty smart head on her shoulders. You've laid the boundaries out, Walsh. I won't step over them, and I won't let Micah know, even though I think you're ultimately wrong about how he'd handle it."

He studies me for a moment, his eyes flickering with uncertainty. Finally, he pulls me back down again and mutters with his lips pressed against my hair. "Let's get some sleep. I'll want to fuck you again before the morning comes."

"Enough already," I say with a giggle. "You're going to wear me out."

His resounding chuckle warms my heart. I know he's conflicted, but it's nice to hear he's still the easily amused Walsh.

My eyes start to droop again, but then I think about something else. "Walsh?"

"Jorie," he returns with annoyance.

"Do you really think I should try to work things out with Vince?"

Normally, Walsh is measured in his responses, taking a moment to process his thoughts. But his answer is swift and adamant, and it makes me smile. "Not while you're in my bed. I don't share."

"Of course, you share." My sarcasm is unmistakable toward the man who belongs to a sex club.

"I don't share *you*," he says adamantly, and warmth blooms in my chest. "Ever."

"Not even if we're at the club together?" I press, wanting to know how proprietary he is of me because it makes me feel good about myself.

"Are you trying to piss me off?" he returns.

"How will I ever know what a threesome is like if you don't show me?" I taunt with a small laugh.

"You're testing my patience," he growls back.

"It's every girl's dream," I say wistfully with a mischievous grin to myself. "Being filled up by two men and having—"

Walsh rolls and flips me to my stomach so fast, I go dizzy from the momentum. Then he's kneeling beside me and pulling me to my knees, positioning my ass in the air. His hand slaps my right cheek with a resounding crack and I yip from the pain, immediately trying to drop back down to the mattress.

"Oh no, you don't," he growls, but I hear the teasing in his voice. "You're getting a lesson and then an orgasm."

I try not to laugh as he pulls me back up, smacks me on my left cheek, and then another slap between my legs like he did at the club. Suddenly, I'm not laughing anymore.

I'm moaning.

God, why do I like that?

"Jesus, Jorie," Walsh says in a rough voice, the teasing completely gone. "You don't know how sexy it is to see my cum leaking out of you."

"Walsh," I whisper and then moan again as his hand goes between my legs. He slips two fingers in me, and I make the mistake of looking over my shoulder at him. He's leaned over, staring in fascination at his fingers working in and out of me. It's so damn hot, and I want to memorialize that look on his face.

His eyes slide to mine, and they're dark and lustful. "Feeling adventurous?"

"With you?" I ask, my voice hoarse with need. "Always."

With a growl of satisfaction, Walsh drags his fingers out of my pussy, pulling his semen up in between my ass cheeks. He rubs his finger around my hole and I hold my breath, waiting for him to enter me. It's not the first time he's had his fingers in my ass. He worked up to three earlier tonight, and I love the feeling.

Absolutely love it.

I also know he's preparing me.

Walsh's hand dips back down, gathers more of the lube he deposited in me not long ago, and one finger easily slides in my ass.

I start to pant and push back against him. I feel his other hand spreading my cheeks, perhaps to get a better view, then he's got two fingers inside me. He moves them in a way that I can feel the stretch. I close my eyes and concentrate on the feeling, listening to Walsh's breaths become more shallow and rough.

Three fingers in and I'm uncomfortably full, and still I push back against him.

"Fuck," he mutters, then his fingers are gone and his cock is pushing inside me slowly. I blow out all the air in my lungs and my instinct has me still pushing back against him, absolutely no fear of what he's doing.

"More," I tell him breathlessly.

He slides in an inch, and it burns oh so fucking good. He waits, and the burn goes away.

"More," I urge him on.

"Mmm," he moans as he slides in a little deeper. "So tight. So perfect."

My chest is heaving, the pressure of the excitement of what he's doing to me almost suffocating.

Walsh's hands come to my ass, and I can feel him pulling my cheeks apart again. I look over my shoulder, and, once again, he's staring in fascination as he enters the one place no man has been before.

He leans his weight against me, sliding all the way in, and I think I want to die from how good it feels. If I thought I had an emotional connection to Walsh before—for saving me when I was bleeding on a bathroom floor or for giving me so much pleasure the last few days—none of that compares to the way I feel about him in this moment.

I've shared something with him that's priceless.

"You okay, Jor?" he asks roughly.

"Yes," I huff out. "You?"

He chuckles, then his eyes come to mine as I continue to look at him over my shoulder. "You have no idea how fucking turned on I am right now." His eyes slide back down to where we're connected. "Seeing my cock stuffed inside your ass."

I can't even answer as he pulls back to the tip and slides gently back into me.

"Oh, God," I moan as I wiggle a little against him.

"Now your ass belongs to me as well," he says in a guttural voice of triumph that I feel all the way down to my clit. It compels me to touch myself, and Walsh starts to move in and out of me.

He takes his time, stays ever so gentle with his movements, and I reach a quick orgasm with my own fingers. Walsh praises my initiative. With a few more strokes, he's filling my ass up with his semen.

We collapse to the bed, and I'm out like a light.

♦

"Jorie, wake up," Walsh calls to me softly.

I feel his lips against mine, and I swat him away. "No more. I'm tired."

Walsh laughs in amusement and then the smell of coffee hits me. I open my eyes and see Walsh fully dressed in slacks and a dress shirt, his hair damp from an obvious shower, sitting on the edge of the bed near my hip. He's holding a cup of steaming coffee in his hands.

I manage a sleepy smile and pull myself up to sit against the headboard, wincing as various aches hit my body, most of which is centered around my ass having been fucked last night.

Or was that this morning?

I've lost track of time.

"Sore, huh?" Walsh asks me with a knowing smirk on his face.

"You absolutely have to leave my ass alone tonight," I mutter as I take the coffee and blow on it.

"Good," he says with a bigger smirk. "I feel like fucking that pretty mouth tonight. We'll work on your deep throating."

I roll my eyes at him and take a delicious sip of java heaven. When I swallow, I ask, "You on your way to work?"

"Got property to buy and things to build," he quips as he looks at his watch, then back to me. "But first, we need to discuss a few things."

"I'm not letting you push me away again," I practically hiss at him.

He grins. "Relax there, hell kitten. I'm not pushing you away."

"Okay," I mutter and take another sip of coffee.

"First," he says as he leans on one hip and reaches into his pocket. He pulls out a sheet of paper. "This is the code to the penthouse elevator. You're welcome here anytime."

Warmth again blooms within me, and I manage to withhold a sappy smile so Walsh doesn't think I'm getting too attached. He puts the paper on the nightstand and I give him a solemn nod, although I'm dancing inside. "Okay. Thanks."

"Second," he says as he places his palm on the mattress near my opposite hip and leans over me. "I need you to call Micah."

"What? Why?" I ask in astonishment.

"He asked me yesterday to get up with you. Check on you."

"He did?"

Walsh nods. "And I'd like you to call him and tell him that I got up with you."

"So he doesn't worry?" I surmise.

"So he doesn't keep pushing at me, which makes me feel like shit that he wants me to check up on you and there's no real need to do that since I'm fucking you," Walsh says, and that makes me wince.

"I'm sorry," I say softly. "I know this is hard."

The expression on his face softens as he leans closer to my face. "One last thing… if you want to work things out with Vince, you need to say the word and I'll step aside. I was being a little selfish last night when—"

My fingers come to his lips, press them closed, and he stops talking.

"I'm right where I want to be," I assure him, and because he still looks troubled by our complicated relationship, I add on, "For now."

Walsh's lips curve into a grateful smile, and I pull my fingers away from his mouth.

Then his lips are on mine, giving me a sweet kiss goodbye. When he pulls back, he says, "Be ready for dinner at seven, here at my apartment. We'll go out and eat, then I'm taking you back to The Wicked Horse."

A pleasant cramp of desire hits me between the legs, but I just nod at him.

Standing from the bed, Walsh looks down at me and says, "Don't forget to call Micah."

"Got it," I assure him with a smart salute.

"Going to spank that pussy again tonight," he says with a grin.

"Looking forward to it, baby," I say with an answering one.

CHAPTER 15

Walsh

I WALK AROUND the 3D mockup of the new shopping center we want to build in Reno, admiring the architect's rendition. He points at the various features, noting areas where we have multiple options that could be changed up to draw in a variety of retailers.

My partners, August Kline and Carina Van DeBosch, also study the model in quiet contemplation as the architect drones on and on.

I don't need to hear it. It's a clever design and we'll get a very good return on our investment. Carina asks a question about the interior greenspace, asking if it can be enlarged to double as a live entertainment venue.

I listen with half an ear and am all too glad when my phone dings in my pocket, indicating a text. I pull it out and smile when I see it is from Jorie.

It merely says, *Pink or Black?*

I look up to see Carina and the architect involved in deep conversation, August listening in, and I send a quick text back to her. *Pink or black what?*

She responds back almost immediately with a picture of two pairs of panties laid out on my bed. One pink, the other black.

Definitely pink.

She writes back. *You know, I only used to wear pink panties when I was fifteen.*

That just gave me a hard-on. I snicker when I hit send.

Perv, she retorts, and then gives me a smiling emoji.

My fingers fly over the screen, typing back to her. *You in the pink panties, nothing else on, spread and waiting for me on my dining room table. I'll be there in thirty minutes.*

I smile in satisfaction as I wait for her response. It's been a damn good week with Jorie. She's stayed at my apartment every night, and we've gone to The Wicked Horse twice. What we do in the privacy of my bedroom is far more intimate than what we do at the club, but I love having her in both places. In my bedroom, she's all soft and pliant with breathy moans and worshipful eyes.

At the club, she's a writhing, screaming mess. She's fucking glorious in her abandonment, and I wonder if she always had that in her, or if I bring it out.

My ego wants to pin the blame squarely on my shoulders.

Can't tonight, she texts back. *Having dinner with Elena.*

I stare at her words and take note of the keen disappointment I can feel in my bones. While we've been together every night this week, we've done nothing more than grab dinner where we tend to find ourselves reminiscing about old times growing up, and then fuck all night. It's what I wanted… that no-strings, casual sex.

And now that I might not see Jorie tonight, the fact I'm feeling bent out of shape about it gives me the wiggins. It scares the fuck out of me that I might have become dependent on Jorie.

Or possibly even addicted.

This scares me because this is how it started with Renee. Off the charts, kinky, dirty, filthy fucking that neither of us could get enough of it. Yes, we were possibly even addicted to each other and for some stupid reason we were never able to figure out, it led us to the altar.

My inner sense of self-preservation tells me to let it go.

Wish her an enjoyable time tonight.

Play it casually.

Instead, I write, *Why don't I take both you ladies out for dinner? Then we'll take in a show or something.*

I hit send, and then curse, "Fuck."

"Something wrong?" August asks me from across the table.

I shake my head. "Just something I need to take care of," I tell him with a casual smile. Then I nod to the model. "But you have my approval to go forward."

August nods at me, then turns back to Carina, who is still talking to the architect with animated hands. She's the detail person in our three-way partnership. She'll hone in on and iron out the nitty-gritty shit that August and I overlook.

My phone dings, and I look down. *That's awesome. What time and how should we dress? I mean... you know... where are we going to dinner? Fancy? Casual? So excited.*

And then she put a little heart emoji on the end.

I grit my teeth and write back without any sense of self-preservation anymore. *Fancy, expensive restaurant. High-dollar cocktails. Put your dancing shoes on.*

God, what am I turning into?

"I GOT TO say, Walsh," Elena yells as she puts her arm around my shoulder and kisses my cheek. "You sure know how to treat the women in your life well."

I smirk down at her as we wait for Jorie to come back from the restroom. We had a three-hour dinner at the best restaurant in Vegas, and then I suggested a nightclub where we could drink and dance. Except, dancing's not really my thing, but I sure didn't mind watching Jorie shake her ass out there with Elena.

"Women?" I yell back at her because the music's shaking the building.

She gives it right back to me just as loud. "You know... as her best friend, I'm your woman, too."

"In the platonic sense, right?"

"God, yes," she says back in horror. "I mean, I'm the

bestie. You get me along for the ride. You hurt her, I destroy you. You buy her Tiffany's, you buy me Tiffany's. See?"

"Got it," I tell her with an amused shake of my head.

The music turns slow, and Elena wags her finger in my face. "No, no, no. I may be the other woman in your life, but you can't slow dance with me. There are some lines I won't cross."

I roll my eyes at her, and then sweep my gaze across the club looking for Jorie. Suddenly, I feel her hands on my hips as she presses into me from behind. I look over my shoulder at her, and she slides around to stand in front of me.

"You about ready to go?" she asks. "It's getting late."

I respond by taking her hand and leading her out onto the dance floor. It's practically empty because no one comes to a Vegas nightclub to slow dance, but I don't give a fuck. I feel like swaying to cheesy music with the hottest woman I've ever been with.

The girl in my life I've known longer than any other.

Jorie's smile is soft and her eyes are sparkling with the champagne she drank earlier as I pull her to me. I bring her hand in close to my chest and wrap the other around her back. She presses her face into my neck, and I fucking love the feel of her breath on my skin.

"This is weird," she murmurs.

"Why's that?" I ask with a smile playing on my lips.

"You being all romantic."

I snicker. "I can be romantic."

"Yes," she deadpans and then mimics me. "That's it, baby, come for me harder. Or, take my cock down your throat, baby, and I'll give you multiples after."

I reach down and pinch her ass hard. Her pelvis flies into mine as she yelps.

"I do not talk like that all the time," I admonish her. "And besides, you like my dirty talk."

I can feel her sigh into my body, and she admits softly. "I really do. I love dirty Walsh."

My step falters slightly at her casual drop of the "L" word, but her tone was teasing enough that I don't take it for anything more than her profession that she's got a kinky side like me.

"You had enough dancing tonight?" I ask.

"Yes, and I'm horny," she says petulantly. My hand goes down to palm her ass, pressing her in tighter so she can feel I'm horny, too. "Want to go fuck in the bathroom?"

This time, I do stumble. When I regain our rhythm, I pull my head back to look down at her. "I've created a monster."

"You didn't create it," she says with a wink. "You just released it."

"Well, as fun as fucking you in the bathroom sounds, I'm thinking tonight I just want you on my mattress, on your back with your feet pressed into my shoulders and my hand over your mouth," I tell her.

"Why a hand over my mouth?" she asks, her head tilted to the side and her green eyes dancing.

"Because Elena is going to be in the guest bedroom as she's had too much to drink tonight, and I don't want her hearing you scream every time I make you come."

Jorie bats her eyelashes at me and simpers, "Oh, Walsh… see… you are a romantic."

"Make fun if you will, but you'll be owing me an apology soon," I warn.

She merely cocks a thin beautiful eyebrow at me in question.

"Reach into my pocket," I tell her.

"I'm not giving you a hand job out here on the dance floor."

"Smartass," I tell her. "My jacket pocket, on the inside."

She shoots me a huge, beautiful grin and her hand dives into the left pocket. She finds it empty, then it dives into the right. When it comes out, she's holding a square Tiffany's box.

"Oh, wow," she says as she looks at it with wide eyes. "You *are* romantic."

"Open it," I tell her as I release my hold and we stand in the middle of the dance floor.

She doesn't waste any time, and then she's gasping at the white-gold chain bracelet with the Tiffany charm attached.

Jorie looks up at me, and it kills me to see a little bit

of confusion in her eyes. I know I'm crossing a line, but I fucking couldn't help myself when I walked by the store, which is in my hotel lobby, after work.

I try to make light of it. "Will I get laid tonight?"

She gives me a glare and then looks back to the bracelet. "It's beautiful."

"Here," I say as I take the jewelry from the box. "Hold up your wrist."

Jorie watches as I put it on her, and then she looks up to me. "Thank you."

"You're welcome," I say, but then I shoot a look over at Elena watching us from the edge of the dance floor. "But tell her I'm not buying her one."

"Huh?" Jorie asks with confusion.

"Inside joke," I tell her as I bring a hand around her neck. I pull her to me and lay a soft kiss on her cheek. "I'll explain it to you later after we fuck."

Jorie laughs and steps into me for an impromptu hug that surprises me as much as it warms me. My heart skips a beat when she says, "There's my Walsh."

CHAPTER 16

Jorie

"WHAT ARE YOU and Walsh doing tonight?" Elena asks me through the phone that I have pressed to my ear. I'm walking around Walsh's apartment, looking for something constructive to do. His housekeeper is too damn good. There's not even a speck of dust for me to swipe up.

"Not sure," I tell her as I saunter into the kitchen. "Maybe I could make dinner for us."

"That would be sweet. Very homemaker-ish. Wear nothing but a frilly apron so when he walks in, he attacks you."

I laugh as I open the refrigerator, taking in the fact there's nothing there but coffee creamer and protein drinks. I shouldn't have expected more… that's what his fridge has looked like for the past few weeks since I've been staying here.

"Never mind," I say glumly as I close the refrigerator door. "I'd have to go grocery shopping and that seems like overstepping my bounds a bit."

"Please, girl," Elena says dismissively. "He's fucking your face. You can make a goddamn meatloaf."

My laugh this time is deep and boob shaking. "God, you crack me up."

"Anymore from Vince?" she asks. I haven't seen Elena in three days—not since I went home to do laundry because Walsh doesn't have a washer and dryer. He uses the hotel laundry service. He offered that to me, but I can't have strangers pawing through my panties.

"He called me yesterday morning," I tell her.

"And?"

"And nothing. It was the same stuff. He's sorry for the things he said, he misses me, he wants me to come home. He doesn't want me to throw away eight years we filled with a lot of great memories."

"How does that make you feel?" Elena asks.

"Like I should be laying on your psychiatry couch, Freud," I tell her dryly as I walk through the kitchen into the living room. I stand before the massive glass wall and look out over Vegas, which isn't so sparkly at four o'clock in the afternoon.

"Seriously, Jorie," she presses. "You're in limbo. You need to shit or get off the pot."

"I don't want to get off the metaphorical pot," I tell her candidly. "I like where I am."

"It will never be more," she reminds me of the one thing that plagues my soul. "You'll always be Walsh's dirty little secret."

"That's harsh," I whisper.

"I'm sorry, sweetie. I just don't want you to get complacent. Fine… burn off some sex calories, explore all the things he can offer. But do it looking forward to your future. You're gorgeous, a great catch, and you want a family someday. You're not going to get that with Walsh."

"I know," I say glumly. "But it's only been a few weeks. I've got years ahead of me."

"You have a husband pushing you to do something."

"I thought you didn't like Vince," I say curiously. She seems to be his champion today.

"I can't stand Vince," she says freely. "But he's right to be making you think about your future."

"I got a job interview set for tomorrow," I say as I change the subject and turn away from the window to start my pacing around Walsh's apartment. I stop in my tracks when I see Walsh standing there just outside the elevator.

Memories of that first night he brought me here play in vivid flashback, and I start walking to him with a little sway in my hips.

"Gotta go," I tell Elena softly. "Walsh is home."

"Wait a minute—" she says, but I disconnect the call. She'll forgive me.

I pocket my phone as I near him, his eyes watching me with dark curiosity.

"You're home early," I murmur as I reach him, my hands going to the belt on his dress slacks. As I start to pull it free, I add, "Looks like you had an exhausting day. Let me make it better for you."

His lips quirk at the lame come on, but he doesn't stop me as I undo his pants after dropping his belt. And Walsh in no way looks like he had a hard day. He looks as fresh and GQ handsome as he did when he left early this morning.

He's thick and hard when I pull him free of his briefs, and I drop to my knees with my hand wrapped around his girth. Without hesitation, I take him in my mouth as I look up at him and start to move. I lick and suck, squeezing and stroking him with my hand. I expect him to take over at any moment now, but he just watches me from above with lust on his face.

It's like that with us always, and I hope to fuck it never changes.

Walsh lets me do my thing. He doesn't take over, but his hands do come up to gently frame my face. I move on him slowly, savoring every little groan I drag out of this normally stoic man. I flutter my tongue on the sensitive underside just below the head of his cock, and press my tongue into the slit. My hand moves his balls, and I gently squeeze them as I work his shaft.

And when he comes with a strangled moan, his hands clutching at my hair, I watch in pure enjoyment as the pleasure washes over his face, hardens his jaw, and makes his throat go taut as he strains with release.

Fucking beautiful.

When he pulls out of my mouth, he yanks me up off the ground, bends over, and throws me into a fireman's carry. He heads straight for the bedroom, and I smile with anticipation.

♦

I COLLAPSE ON top of Walsh, my heart hammering because that was some intense shit. The normally in control alpha man came home today with the idea in mind to let me play. He let me blow him in slow fashion, and then he put me in a straddle over his waist on the bed, lowering me down slowly onto his cock after he recuperated while he ate me out.

It was perfect. I rode him slowly at first, but then the lust and need took over and I bounced up and down on him with abandonment as I made all kinds of gibberish sounds.

Walsh's hands come to stroke my lower back gently as we let our systems cool down, our breathing come back to normal, and our hearts to get out of stroke territory.

When he rolls me to my side and faces me, I give him a smile. "You're home early."

"It was a slow day at the office," he says, and I wonder what that means. Did he just make hundreds of thousands of dollars in property deals, or millions? He's so damn successful, but I don't really know what that means.

"What do you want to do tonight?" I ask. I don't tell him I wanted to make him dinner because it smacks of domesticity too much, and I don't want him to think I'm wanting more.

But God, I want more from him. These last few weeks have taken the fond love I've had for this man over the years, mixed it with the deepest intimacy I've ever experienced in my life, and intensified it into something that's beyond description.

Elena was right to push at me, but I'm afraid to move. What I want from Walsh isn't going to happen according to him. He's too set on the fact that Micah won't approve. Of course, I could just approach Micah on the sly and tell him what's going on. The abbreviated, PG version so he doesn't want to kill Walsh, but Micah loves me. He wants me to be happy.

If I did that, though, it would break the trust Walsh has in me. We agreed this would be our secret, and Walsh kept the secret of what happened that night to me all these years. I can't do that to him.

I note that Walsh doesn't answer me, so I prod him with a sassy grin. "Netflix and chill?"

He smiles back at me, but it doesn't fully reach his eyes. "How come you didn't tell me Vince called?"

I'm so stunned by this change of subject that for a moment I can't figure out how he knows that. Then it hits me... he must have been standing outside that elevator for a few minutes and heard my conversation with Elena.

The answer to his question hits me hard, though, and I gently chastise. "Come on, Walsh... you have to know it's hard to talk about one man while fucking another."

I expect him to be ashamed a little, but he pointedly reminds me, "Not if there aren't strings attached to the one man. Besides, we're still friends, right?"

"Um... yeah. Sure," I tell him hesitantly and with a little pain throbbing in the center of my chest. "Yesterday morning, and he's been texting."

Walsh studies me for a moment, and I feel like his words are carefully measured when he says, "I don't want to stand in the way of your marriage.

"You're not," I hastily assure him.

My eyes drop to Walsh's chest and my fingers come up to skim over the hard planes. When I look back up to him, I say, "I need you to let me have this for a while without pressure about Vince. I'm trying to figure myself out, and I'm happy right where I am. I know this is only 'for now' and not 'forever,' but I'm just not ready to give him a chance. I'm not sure I ever will."

In fact, if I had to go with my deepest gut instinct, it's over between me and Vince. I'd like to think I'd fight for my marriage, and Vince was right... we had a lot of great memories. But we have one inherent difference I can't get over. Forget about the sex issue. He doesn't want kids, and I'm not sure that will ever change about him. If I had to have one serious talk with Vince about the future of our marriage, it would be about that, and I'm convinced that's not changed. Every function we'd ever been at together, he always sneered at the little kids, shied away from holding a baby, and mocked his friends who were going through teenager woes. He just doesn't like kids, and that's intolerable to me.

Another moment of silence, and then Walsh nods. I pretend not to notice that I think I saw a flicker of relief in his eyes over my words, because that would give me too much hope.

"You have a job interview tomorrow?" he asks.

I nod. "With the local paper in Henderson. It's still a copyediting position, which I'm not fond of, but it's a way to make some income while I continue to look around."

"You're looking to stay in Henderson?" he asks.

"For now," I return vaguely. I didn't dare look for anything in Vegas, because while Walsh has opened his home freely to me, I don't want it to appear I want or expect more. I know there's nothing that will scare him off faster.

"I have some contacts with some local media here in Vegas if you want me to reach out," he says, and this surprises me.

I try not to read too much into it, so I just say,

"Thanks. That would be awesome."

His smile is bigger, and I don't know what that means either. I take care not to get hopeful, because I have a feeling Walsh could crush me.

Vince hurt me. Shamed me.

But Walsh will destroy me if I don't keep a tight lock on my heart.

"Let's order in dinner," Walsh suggests. "And then watch movies."

"Netflix and chill," I say again with a grin.

"You know that means sex, right?" he asks.

I blink at him in confusion. I'd heard the term a lot, and I just thought it meant chilling on the couch and watching movies.

But I'm okay with the sex, too. "Of course, I know that means sex. Duh… what did you think I thought it meant?"

Walsh barks out a laugh and leans forward to give me a hard kiss. It's one of my favorite things about him… when I amuse him to the point of spontaneous displays of pure affection. Not saying that it's better than the orgasms he gives me, but it feels damn good.

Rolling over, Walsh snags his phone off the nightstand and does a quick check of his messages. He may be technically out of the office, but the man never stops working.

After a few moments, he turns to look at me with a grim look on his face. "Micah texted a little bit ago. He's coming to Vegas this weekend to visit."

"Oh," I say as conflicted feelings overwhelm me. I'm beyond excited to see my brother. We visited each other regularly when I was in L.A. and he was in San Francisco. But it's been a few months and I would love to see him.

On the other hand, that means Walsh and I will have to cool it with each other, and that just plain sucks. We'll also have to pretend and put on an act, and that sucks as well. The secret Walsh and I kept about the night I was attacked was easy. This is going to be much harder.

"I'm going to need you to go back to Elena's for the weekend," he says, and I hate the slightly icy tone in his voice.

"Yeah, absolutely," I say quietly. "Not a problem."

Walsh's expression softens, and he pulls me too him. "It's just for a weekend, okay?"

"Of course," I say with a cheery smile that strains my cheek muscles to make it. "It's totally fine."

CHAPTER 17

Walsh

"WANT ANOTHER DRINK?" I ask Micah as he lounges on my couch and takes the final swallow of his scotch. He flew in about an hour ago, and we're waiting for Jorie to arrive to go out to dinner tonight. My nerves are on edge. I definitely want another drink.

"Nah, man," Micah says as he pushes up from the couch and moves to take his glass back into the kitchen that opens straight from the living room. "Tonight's not about getting drunk. It's about hanging out with my two favorite people in the world."

I smile at him and nod, my stomach clenched.

"But just so you know," he says with a laugh. "Jorie's my first favorite, you're my second."

"As it should be," I reply, and hope that sounds casual enough.

Micah rinses his glass out and sets it on the counter. As he walks back into the living room, he says, "And besides… I figure tomorrow night, you and I are going to hit the town, right?"

"You know it," I say as I push up from the chair, head straight to the wet bar, and replenish my vodka. There is not enough alcohol in the world to get me through this weekend. I take a healthy slug as soon as I cap the bottle.

"Dying to go to The Wicked Horse," Micah says with excitement in his voice. "Want to meet Jerico, too. He and I have been emailing about testing out some more of my designs in his club. Plus, you and me, dude… we haven't had a woman together in a long time. Your stories about the stocks… we've got to hit that, man."

My shoulders tighten and my gut rolls with nausea. How in the fuck I am going to weasel out of this is beyond me, but I've got to figure something out. I don't want another fucking woman other than Jorie.

"Walsh?" Micah says in question, and I turn to look at him. "We good with going there tomorrow night?"

"Damn straight we are," I say with a smile. "A night of debauchery for the both of us."

Fuck, fuck, fuck.

Just then, the elevator doors give a slight hiss as they open, and Jorie is standing there. She looks fucking amazing, wearing a dress done in large black-and-white zebra stripes that's loosely belted around her waist and comes down to her knees. She's got on a pair of sexy-as-shit taupe heels to go with it and my mouth waters as I take in what they do to her legs. Hair in that sleek, angled bob that hangs halfway in between her jaw and shoulders, and that thick crop of bangs straight across her eyebrows make her green eyes brighter than ever.

I swallow hard and try to appear casual.

Her eyes go immediately to Micah, and she gives a squeal of excitement. He rushes to her, picks her up, and swings her around. The skirt of her dresses rises a bit in the back, and I look away guiltily.

"God, I missed you, squirt," Micah says with a choked voice. My guilt intensifies over the naked display of love and affection he has for his sister.

Jorie's voice quavers with equal love. "I missed you, too."

She hugs him hard and looks over his shoulder at me. Her eyes are wary and nervous.

When Micah releases her, I step up and casually say, "Got a hug for me?"

It's a shameless move to touch her, but not something that would raise Micah's eyebrows. I've hugged Jorie a million times over our lives together growing up.

"It's good to see you again," she says to me as she walks into a very brotherly hug. I make the mistake of inhaling her scent, and I'm hit with a jolt of lust for her.

After we quickly release each other, she steps back and surveys my apartment as if it's her first time. She told Micah we met for breakfast one day, but he sure as shit doesn't know I've fucked her on almost every piece of furniture in this apartment. He'll never know she went to her knees right where we're standing in front of the elevator and swallowed every drop of cum I gave her.

Fuck, fuck, fuck.

I have an overwhelming urge to fake a stomachache, a migraine, a goddamn stroke for all I care at this moment, and beg off from this entire weekend.

Instead, I put a smile on my face and tell them, "Come on. We've got prime seats in Moulineaux tonight. I've not eaten there yet, but heard it's amazing."

Jorie smiles back at me before turning to hook her arm through Micah's. She leans over and puts her head on his arm as she's too short to reach his shoulder. They both stroll into the elevator.

This night can't get over with fast enough for me.

♦

"God, I'm stuffed," Jorie says as she licks the last of her chocolate mousse off her spoon and thank God, we're sitting at the table so no one can see my arousal. I'm not sure what it says about me that I've been like this most of the night, just sitting across the table from this beautiful creature.

"This was really good," Micah says in agreement as he pushes his own empty dessert flute away. He picks up his scotch, which I think might be his fourth of the night, and swirls it around before taking a sip. So much for not drinking tonight.

When he sets it back down, he turns to Jorie and asks, "Have you decided on anything with Vince?"

I immediately tense up at the personal question leveled at his sister right out of the blue, and I guess the liquor is making him too loose with his words.

"We've talked a little," she says easily, but I notice the tightness just around the corners of her mouth. "He wants me to come back."

Micah doesn't know the details of what happened. Only Elena and I know Vince kicked her out of the home because he didn't like her performance in bed. Jorie only told him that they separated per Vince's request and he asked her to leave.

"And are you?" Micah presses her.

Her eyes cut to mine before going back to her brother. "Now's probably not the best time to talk about it."

"Why not?" Micah says, turning to look to me for a moment, then back to Jorie. "I'm your brother. Walsh is as good as a brother. We care about you."

God, I want to shoot myself.

Jorie nods and gives a confident smile. "Well, okay… in that case, I don't think I'm interested in reconciling. I've been using this time on my own to evaluate what I want, and I'm pretty sure it's not marriage to Vince."

"He hurt you," Micah says tenderly. "I get that. Some things can't be undone."

Jorie's eyes turn soft as they soak in her brother's

words, and then I'm fucking ripped wide open when she says, "Vince doesn't want children. We might have been able to repair everything else, but it's something I very much want one day."

Micah's hand crosses the table and takes Jorie's. He squeezes it and leans toward her. "You would make a fucking fantastic mother. You get back out there, find the love of your life, and make beautiful babies, okay? I can't wait to be an uncle."

Jorie's smile back to him is bright, and there's no tightness at all around her mouth now. "I will, Micah. I promise."

I swear to God I'm going to throw up. How could I not know this about Jorie? I've had my cock in her ass, my cum in her pussy, but I didn't know how she strongly she wanted children. I mean… I assumed she might, but I had no clue it was a bone of contention with her husband. It goes far deeper than I ever imagined.

Moreover, how in the hell can I keep this up with her when she wants so much out of life, and I can't be the one to give it to her?

But man, if we had babies together, they'd be stunning.

I shake my head and stand up from the table in a little lurch. My head swims with the implications of what I'm doing with Jorie and what she's failing to get. Vince is a non-issue to me now. I'd worried I was perhaps blocking her from her soul mate or something, but it's clear he's not the guy for her.

It's even clearer I'm not the guy, either. Or at least, I can't be that guy for her. Micah wouldn't understand.

Or would he? my subconscious pipes up.

I ignore it and toss my napkin on my chair. "I'm going to use the restroom. Be right back."

Both Micah and Jorie smile at me. Micah totally nonplussed, but I can see the worry for me in Jorie's eyes. She knows that conversation just bothered me, but I can never tell her how much or why.

I make my way through the restaurant to where the restrooms are located. I do nothing more than splash chilly water on my face and stare at myself in the mirror, telling me to get my shit together. This shouldn't be this hard.

But I once told Jorie she was complicated, and it appears that is the understatement of the fucking millennium.

With a sigh, I take a towel from the attendant, dry my face and hands, and put a five-dollar bill in the tip jar. He bobs his head and says, "Thank you, sir. Enjoy the rest of your evening."

Yeah, that's not going to fucking happen, but I smile back at him as I leave.

I come to a dead halt as I find Jorie there waiting for me in the alcove that separates the restrooms from the open restaurant layout.

"What are you doing here?" I ask her as I take her arm and step toward the wall, further shielding us from the patrons.

"Checking on you," she says quietly. "I know this is hard—"

"It's fine," I assure her. "It's fine, and Micah doesn't suspect anything."

"I want to tell him," Jorie says suddenly.

I look left and right; the coast is clear, and I lean into her. "We agreed not to, Jorie. Don't do this to me."

"He'd understand," she promises.

"He wouldn't," I return.

"Walsh—"

"Jorie," I snap. "You know that dildo machine in The Wicked Horse?"

She nods back at me, lips pressed tight.

"Your brother designed it," I tell her in a low voice. "I took a picture of your fine ass as that dildo hammered into you, and I texted it to Micah so he could see his machine in action."

Jorie's mouth falls open in stunned surprise.

"You think he's going to appreciate the fact that was his sister I was exploiting? Fuck... I sent that picture to him knowing he'd probably jack off to it. How do you think that's going to make him feel?"

"Oh, God," she says as her eyes practically glaze over from the implications and she stumbles back to rest against the wall.

"Leave it be, Jorie," I beg. "Please let's just get through this weekend."

She nods at me, her eyes still a little blank. It shreds me up seeing her look so lost.

I press into her. For a moment, I don't give a fuck about Micah. I brush my lips over hers and whisper, "It will be fine. I promise."

"Okay," she whispers back.

But we both know that's a lie, no matter how this turns out.

CHAPTER 18

Jorie

I LOOK AT myself in the full-length mirror that's attached to the back of the bathroom door and appraise myself. Sexy lingerie, high heels, and beach-blown hair. My lips painted cherry red because I know Walsh gets off on that if he wants me to suck his dick.

I turn and grab my phone from the vanity, turn back and take a selfie of myself. I then walk into the bedroom. Perching on the end of the bed, I cross my legs and send the photo to Walsh. It's just past one in the morning. I'm not sure if he'll see it or not, but I hope he's awake.

I type in a few words to follow the photo. *I'm in room 4309.*

You see, I didn't get in my car and drive back to Henderson like I told Micah and Walsh I was going to do. We didn't get in until close to midnight, and they both wanted me to stay at Walsh's so I didn't have to drive back to Henderson. I purposely didn't drink tonight, so they couldn't worry about my ability to make it.

But I'd had this planned.

I was going to be with Walsh tonight come hell or high water.

Pushing up from the bed, I walk over to the windows that look out at the twinkling lights of the strip. I used to hate Vegas, but not so much anymore.

How could I when Walsh is here? When his life's work is located right in the heart of Sin City?

The longer I look out the window, and the longer I wait for his response, the more I dwell on the things that he said to me at the restaurant.

I can't believe Micah made that machine. He's a fucking highly sought-after engineer who is making mechanical fuck machines. The idea repulses me as much as remembrance of riding that thing with Walsh watching excites me. I want to do it again, and we haven't in the times we've been back to The Wicked Horse, because there's been too much other stuff to explore.

My gut clenches as I remember the pain in Walsh's voice tonight when he admitted to sending that photo to Micah. Not knowing who I was, wanting Micah to be excited about it.

I don't let it sicken me, though. The experience with Walsh was beautiful. He had no clue it was me, so it was an innocent mistake in sending it to my brother. It kills me to know that this has been weighing on him, and I really want to be with him tonight so I can reiterate that. I can't stand the thought of him being weighed down so heavily about this.

As minutes tick by and I don't get a response, I assume Walsh is just asleep.

Or he's ignoring you because he's calling it quits, that stupid fucking voice in my head says slyly.

Tears spring to my eyes as I think about losing Walsh, and I know I'll do anything to prevent that. Even if it means I can never tell Micah about our relationship.

Even if it means I'll be nothing more to him than a secret.

It's better than nothing as far as I'm concerned. Seeing the misery on Walsh's face and hearing the burden in his voice made it clear to me that Micah cannot know about us.

The knock on the door startles me and my heart rate accelerates. There's no one it can be other than Walsh.

I drop my phone on the chair by the window and quickly walk to the door. Taking a deep breath, I open it. He stands there... eyes crackling with pent-up frustration and lust. His gaze roams hungrily over my body, then I'm in his arms and he's carrying me to the bed.

He's eerily quiet as he strips the silk and satin from my body, ignoring my shoes. He pulls me to the end of the bed, drops to his knees, and eats me out like he's starving. I shudder and cry out a quick release, but he doesn't stop. He devours me again, going rougher. Shoving fingers in my pussy, getting them wet, and then shoving them in my ass.

I come a second time, arching into the pleasure and crying out his name.

Walsh is then up, stripping his clothes off with lightning speed. I use the moment to crawl back onto the bed, my legs spread open wantonly with blatant invitation.

He takes it. Crawling up my body, raising and spreading my legs before driving into me with brutal force. It hurts and it doesn't. I quickly adjust as he starts moving within me. That beautiful face of his awash with ecstasy. Those golden eyes locked onto mine.

For a moment, he looks down and I think it might be in shame, but it's to further his lust. He watches his cock pounding in and out of me. I drop my gaze there, too, and it's sensory overload as I watch him fuck me.

Walsh brings a thumb to my clit, presses down on it, and I can feel the sensation from his cock on the other side of it. Three, maybe four hard strokes from Walsh and I'm bursting apart again.

With glazed eyes, Walsh looks back to me. His breathing harsh, his jaw locked tight. I see he's close, then he's pulling out of me and coming all over my stomach and breasts with a long groan of release. It's so fucking sexy. I always feel like he's marking me as his when he does that.

When he's empty, he pushes his cock back into me. He moves his hips gently, tiny little shudders still coursing through both of us.

Finally, he stops moving and runs a finger through the semen on my skin. Without a word, he brings it to my mouth and rubs it on my lips. I lick after him, wanting his mellow taste on my tongue.

He smiles at me with such tenderness, my heart pulses with joy. Then he pulls out and heads into the bathroom. He returns with a wet cloth, cleans me off, and tosses it to the floor before crawling onto the mattress and pulling me into his arms.

"Is Micah asleep?" I ask him.

"I think so," he says back quietly.

We lay together, arms wrapped tight, and I know this evening is playing on rewind in our minds. I take the moment to reassure him. "I won't ever tell him, Walsh. I promise. This is just between you and me forever. Even if you're done with me, I'll never tell."

Walsh squeezes me hard and mutters, "Christ, Jorie… I don't think I can ever be done with you."

"I don't want to be done with you, either," I whisper.

"But you want things that—"

"Don't say it," I break into his thoughts urgently. "All you need to know is that I want you and that is more than I could want for anything right now."

I trail off, not quite done telling him what I need to in order to reassure him. But there are bottled feelings inside of me, wanting to break loose, so I add on, "I love—"

Walsh rears up and looks down at me with hard eyes. "Don't you dare say that, Jorie. Don't even think it. You say that to me, and I'll want to tell Micah. I'll want to destroy him to have you, and you can't put me in that situation."

"Okay," I tell him quickly. "Okay. I won't tell you."

Walsh's eyes fill with pain, and he drops his forehead to mine. "This is so fucked up, baby. So goddamn fucked up."

My arms go around this man I love. I love him still in all the ways I used to, and I love him more for all the things he's given me. But I keep that inside, and I'm truly okay with not saying it to him. I don't need to. Walsh's reaction tells me he already knows.

His proclamation that he'd be willing to destroy his relationship with Micah also tells me he loves me, too.

I let that be enough for now.

Perhaps over time, we can come up with a way to make this work. It would deepen the lie, but maybe Walsh can revisit the subject with Micah in a more old-fashioned approach. We could remold the lie and start over. He could tell Micah he wants to ask me out on a date and would like his permission.

It seems so sordid all these webs we've woven, but it could work. Micah would never know about me at The Wicked Horse. He wouldn't blame Walsh for having me there.

"What are you thinking?" Walsh asks as he lifts his head up and stares down at me.

"I'm thinking that you and I have a really good thing going right now," I tell him with as much confidence as I can muster up. "It will be fine. We'll be fine. I promise."

The smile of relief that comes to Walsh's face tells me that this is the right path.

For now.

"Listen," Walsh says, and I can tell by the tone of his voice he hates what he's about to tell me. "Micah wants me to take him to The Wicked Horse."

My eyes flare wide as I never considered this possibility. I assumed, wrongly, that the three of us would hang out again.

Oh, God.

Oh… God.

"Jorie," Walsh says urgently but I barely hear him. "I swear to you I won't do anything. I don't want to do anything with anyone but you."

I try to wiggle out from his hold, but his arms lock tight around me.

"Jorie," Walsh says as he brings a hand to my jaw, forcing me to turn my head to face him. "I swear to fucking God, you've got nothing to worry about with me. But I can't say no to him. I promised he could talk to Jerico, the owner. They want to talk business, and well… before you and I started, Micah had me promise

I'd take him on his next visit. He's already asked about it."

"Oh, God," I mutter out loud this time and try to pull away from Walsh. His arms again lock tight, but then they immediately loosen when he hears the hysteria in my voice. "Let me go, please. I need some space."

Walsh releases me, and I roll from the bed. I feel completely vulnerable right now, so I grab my small duffle and pull out a t-shirt and panties. I quickly don them and turn to face Walsh, who still sits unabashedly naked on the bed. His expression is worried as he watches me like a hawk.

I take a deep breath, and let it out. "I don't want you going there without me."

"I don't want to go there without you," Walsh says, and I can hear the truth in his voice. "But I have to. It's for one night, and I'll fake a fucking migraine or something so he won't expect me to participate—"

"Wait," I practically screech. "Participate? You would participate with Micah?"

"With another woman," he clarifies, and that makes it even worse.

"Oh, God," I say again with a trembling voice. "I don't think I can handle this. Have you done that before with Micah?"

"Yes," is all he provides me.

"And he expects you tomorrow, to what?" I ask tremulously. "Fuck a woman with him?"

"He'll expect it, but I won't," Walsh says firmly as he rolls out of bed and comes to stand before me. God, he's so fucking beautiful and perfect.

"It's a lot of temptation," I say angrily. "And let's face it, you don't want Micah to know about us, so why wouldn't you do that just to make sure he's got no suspicions?"

Damn, I know I sound completely unhinged right now, but I seriously am having a fit of jealousy so powerful I can't seem to calm down.

"Jorie," Walsh snaps at me as he takes me by the shoulders. "Do you trust me?"

"Yes," I say automatically.

Well, shit… I feel that deep in my bones. I do trust him.

"Then trust me when I say, I'll be thinking about you the entire time. I will be faithful to you. I'll come back and when Micah is asleep, I'll come to you in this same room and fuck some reassurance into you."

The tears well up in my eyes, and Walsh looks crushed by my reaction. He pulls me into him hard and wraps his arms around me.

"Fuck it," he growls before pressing a hard kiss to the top of my head. "I'll back out of it. I'll figure a way to get Micah there without me."

Overwhelmingly deep love courses through me for Walsh, and the lengths he'd go to assuage something as stupid as jealousy.

I shake my head adamantly and pull back to look at him. "No. Don't. I'll be fine. I trust you."

"I'll do whatever you want me to, Jorie."

"Go with Micah," I say even though I still can't stand the thought of it. "He expects it, and we don't want him suspicious."

Walsh pulls me back to the bed, and then makes love to me slowly. While our first fucking was all about the feelings and the orgasm, this time Walsh spends an extraordinary amount of time telling me just how much he wants me, how beautiful I am, how no one compares to me.

Every word is a balm to my heart because I take it from him with the knowledge that I know he loves me. I just have to figure out how I can have him without any secrets, and not ruin his relationship with my brother in the process.

CHAPTER 19

Walsh

THIS IS ABSOLUTE torture.

It must be what hell is like.

I sit at the bar in The Silo and nurse a ginger ale, mainly to keep the ruse going that I'm too under the weather to participate with Micah. He seemed to accept it, and I think that had something to do with the fact he easily found a woman who agreed to use the dildo machine with him.

Now I watch him in action. I can't see clearly as he's drawn a crowd around the glass wall, but I see enough to know what he's doing, and I can't lie… it turns me on. It turns me on because I remember Jorie on that machine and I've fantasized about getting her back on it.

We got here about an hour ago and, within two minutes, I was ready to leave. But Jerico met us and of course, Micah had to get the grand tour. They chatted easily about some of the designs Micah was working on, but I only listened with half an ear. I was too busy feeling guilty about being here in the first place.

I shouldn't be here without Jorie.

I know some couples swing without each other in attendance, but I don't want to fucking swing. I might be a pussy for admitting it, but I just don't want anyone but her. If this clusterfuck ever gets outed, or Jorie decides she's had enough and wants to move on to a better prospect, then I'm not sure how I get over having someone like her.

We finally came to The Silo, as Jerico saved it for last so Micah could watch his machine in action. Micah was spectacularly proud—he should be—but immensely turned on. He had an erection popping the front of his dress slacks while we watched and discussed potential modifications.

And I can't lie about that either. Watching the machine being used, remembering it with Jorie, and listening to Jerico and Micah talking about how he could make a variety of attachments to mount on the piston had me sporting wood too. I was horny as fuck for Jorie, and I couldn't wait to get the fuck out of here and meet her in the hotel room that sits sixteen stories beneath my penthouse apartment.

"He's got some really clever ideas," Jerico says as he sits down on a stool beside me. "Those machines could be high dollar too."

I shrug as I watch Micah through the glass. He's got a woman on the machine, and he's playing with the remote. I can hear her screams of pleasure, and my dick gets a little harder.

"He makes a lot of money through his engineering firm," I point out. "This is just a hobby for him."

"I don't think so," Jerico says, and that catches my attention. I turn to look at him. "I think he's considering doing this full time. Design and then mass production."

"You're shitting me?" I ask in astonishment. I mean, Micah likes kinky shit, but I didn't know it was his passion.

Jerico turns and I do the same, both of us watching Micah, who is now unbuttoning his pants. The woman is getting jackhammered by the dildo, which has obviously been exchanged out for a new one after the last woman was on it.

"I offered to stake him the money if he wants to do it," Jerico says, and my head again snaps back to him. He doesn't look at me though, merely watching Micah in action for a few moments.

I'm completely stunned. I thought Micah was like me. Professional by day, kinky bastard by night. The thought of him moving into the sex industry full time is a shocker for sure and not necessarily the best decision in my opinion. I'm not sure Jorie is going to like this either.

Micah catches my attention again back in the glassed room. He's naked now and kneels to make an adjustment on the seat. It raises the woman a bit higher, and tilts so her ass sticks out. The dildo continues fucking her from underneath the seat's opening.

He makes another adjustment, I believe pulling the pistoning arm back a bit, and her ass moves back even more. There's no mistaking his intention.

I sip at my ginger ale, missing Jorie so much I ache, and incredibly turned on because Micah is doing to that woman what I want to do to his sister. We'd even talked about doing a re-creation of our first night together on that machine. Jorie's ass accommodates me beautifully now, so she suggested moving it to the next level on one of our visits to the club.

That would be a special visit for sure. Jorie and I had cut our time here back to barely once a week. Neither of us needed the stimulation the club provided, our attraction and desire for one another keeping us constantly fueled.

I'd give anything right now to just have her in my empty apartment, chilling out on the couch and watching Netflix.

And fucking before we went to sleep, of course.

I watch with growing discomfort as Micah takes the woman's ass as roughly as the machine is giving it to her. But I know it's okay because I've seen that woman in here plenty and she likes it that way. I've seen her do double anal without so much as blinking.

Right now, she's screaming out in ecstasy and shuddering as her body is wracked with orgasms. Micah's head falls back as he comes inside of her, and my dick gets harder as I watch him slowly move in and out of her ass while he amps up the speed of the dildo in her pussy.

She screams and comes again.

"He'll make a killing off those machines," Jerico murmurs, his eyes pinned on Micah.

I can't say I disagree. Fuck, I'd like to have one installed in my apartment so Jorie could ride it every night.

"Now," Jerico says as he stands from the stool. "I'm completely fucking horny for Trista. I'm heading out, but tell Micah I'll follow up with him during the week to discuss this more."

I reach a hand out, and Jerico shakes it. "Sure thing. See you around."

"Will I?" Jerico says with a grin. "You're never here anymore and I only see you with that dark-haired beauty you won't share with anyone."

Christ, I didn't realize Jerico had seen me here with Jorie. He's almost never here when I am to begin with and when Jorie and I come in, we do our thing and then leave.

"I've not seen her, but Larissa told Trista who told me," he explains as if he could read my mind. "I hate to lose one of my most popular patrons, but I wish you the best, buddy."

"Thanks," I say with a dry throat and a jerk of my chin in acknowledgment.

Jerico leaves, and I'm thankful he hasn't seen Jorie. He'd be able to tell she was Micah's sister in a heartbeat.

My head starts throbbing… an honest-to-goodness headache that makes my boner deflate. Now that Micah got his rocks off, I'm hoping we can head back to my apartment. He's got a morning flight out, and I know he won't want to stay out too late.

I just really need to be with Jorie right now, if for nothing other than to make the most of our time together.

♦

I SLIP INTO the hotel room, and I can tell by the utter silence that Jorie's asleep. I didn't get out of The Wicked Horse as early as I'd planned. Micah wanted to fuck on The Deck. I was thankfully able to use my slight "vertigo" problem to beg off. I'd not had an episode in years, but he doesn't know that. I don't fuck out on The Deck mainly for that reason, so it wasn't an out-and-out lie.

I had told Micah I was going to explore the other rooms, so he probably thought I'd had sex with someone despite my "stomach issue". This was fine by me.

We didn't talk about it on the way home because he was trashed. He passed out face down on the guest bed, and I felt confident I could slip away to be with Jorie. I made a mental note to ask Jorie if she thought Micah was drinking too much lately. It was starting to become a concern, but then again… it didn't seem to affect his regular life so I wasn't sure.

I take off my clothes and slide into the bed, spooning up behind her. I know instantly she's awake by how stiff she is in my arms. I pull her in closely and whisper, "I'm so fucking glad to be here right now."

She responds by wiggling her ass against my dick. It starts to respond, and I mutter, "Yes, I'm horny from watching that stuff all night, and yes, I want to fuck you, but for now… let me just hold you for a bit, okay?"

"Was it awful?" she asks, her voice carrying concern for me hanging out in a sex club all night. That's whacked.

"It was hell, baby," I tell her softly.

"I couldn't sleep," she says into the darkness.

"I know." My arms lock tighter around her. "I won't ever go there again without you."

"Deal," she says softly, and I think all is okay.

"In fact," I add on. "I'm okay if we don't go back there again."

This surprises her, and she wiggles in my embrace so she can flip around and face me. I can't see her features very well, but the tone of her voice tells me that makes her wary.

"Why not?"

"I don't need it to have it bad for you, Jorie," I explain. "I've got it bad for you 24/7."

"It's fun, but I don't need it either," she says, and my body relaxes. "Maybe only for special occasions."

I chuckle. "And one last hoorah to get you on that

machine. I want that again."

"Mmm," she murmurs as she drops her hand down to my cock. Her warm hand starts to stroke me as she whispers, "I want that again, too."

My hand goes between her legs, and she's perfectly wet for me. "Missed this tonight. Fantasized about this tonight."

"It's yours every night," she says. For a moment, I imagine a world I could have Jorie in my future for real. Where I could be open about it and not keep her like a dirty little secret from her brother.

Pulling my hand out from between her legs, I toss the covers off us and roll to my back. My hand goes to her head. "Get those lips on my cock."

She sits up, goes to her knees, and immediately leans over me. She takes me in deep and has gotten so fucking good, she can swallow the tip of my dick now without any reaction. She does so now, and a grunt of pleasure escapes me. I allow myself just a moment of pure bliss in this woman's mouth, then my hands are on her hips and I'm dragging her over me.

She doesn't need any encouragement. We've sixty-nined several times before, trying out a variety of positions. This is my favorite though because she lowers her pussy to my face and rubs herself all over my mouth. Jorie has blossomed and isn't afraid to ask for what she wants. She sure as fuck isn't afraid to give.

My tongue drives in deep as I use my hands on her

hips to help move her on me. I take breaths of air when I can, allow myself to feel her on my dick, and I eat her out hard. Best fucking meal in the world in my opinion.

It doesn't take her long, but then again, it never does. I'm always a little stunned and totally full of myself how fast I can get her off, but she's always super reactive to my tongue. She explodes, grinds down on me, and scrapes her teeth up my cock at the same time.

Fuck, that feels good.

I let her barely lick me for a few moments as she experiences the full orgasm, but once the tremors die away, she's back on my cock again. In deep, her throat clamping tight to the tip each time. Jorie's hand goes to my balls and I close my eyes, giving in to nothing but sensation while I casually pet her sensitive clit. I think about putting my mouth back on her, but honestly... Jorie's so good at sucking my cock now, I just want to experience it. I'll get her off again after.

Pulling all the way off me, she whispers in the dark, "Raise your legs up and spread them for me, Walsh."

This is new, but I don't hesitate to comply. There isn't anything I wouldn't do for her when it comes to sex.

I can't see what she's doing as her pussy's blocking by view, but then her warm mouth is back on me, working my shaft.

Then I feel her finger pressing against my hole, and I can't fucking help but tense. It's wet and warm, I'm assuming from a trip to her mouth before she took me back in.

She bobs her head faster, her hand stroking my balls. I relax, give into the feeling for a few blissful moments, and then she's pushing that delicate finger straight into my ass.

I bark out a cry of surprise and pleasure all at the same time, and I'm completely unprepared for the orgasm that rips through me. Jorie hums in appreciation as she sucks me down, gently moving her finger in and out as I continue to come and come and come.

"Holy fuck," I groan, my hips rising off the bed to get more of her mouth? More of her finger? I have no fucking clue, but that was some intense shit.

When I'm absolutely spent, she pulls off me and gently slides her finger out.

"Jesus, Jorie," I mutter. "You're a fucking dirty girl."

"I've been reading," she says, and I can hear the satisfied smirk in her tone.

"You deserve another orgasm for that," I tell her as I pull her back down onto my face, and she sighs with contentment.

CHAPTER 20

Jorie

WALSH KNOCKS ON the bathroom door again and impatiently calls out, "Come on, Jorie. It seriously can't take you that long to get ready."

I giggle and look at Elena as she glues the last feather in place. We'd commandeered his master bathroom tonight so I could recreate my outfit from the night we first met at the club, down to the last peacock feather. Elena gladly volunteered to help get me ready, and I can't wait to see his face.

I can't wait to get on that machine tonight at The Wicked Horse. We're going in sort of thinking this is our last time for a while, and then we're going to step back from the club and just have each other. I feel it's the right thing to do while we establish this weird relationship of ours.

Micah flew out early this morning. I miss him already, but there's also a sense of relief that he's gone. That I can be with Walsh and be free about it at the same time. That doesn't mean that I won't give up hope that I can have it all; it's just right now I'm focused on taking this one day at a time.

And today—or rather tonight—Walsh is going to put me right back on that machine that started this all.

"We'll be out in a few minutes," I call back to him, and he groans in frustration.

Elena laughs quietly and whispers, "You're a lucky bitch to have a man who pushes every one of your buttons in the right way, you know that, right?"

"Right," I say with a firm nod of my head.

"You realize now, Vince was wrong about you," she says as her fingertips smooth the feather she just placed down.

I look at her through the mirror over the vanity and shake my head slightly. "I don't know that he was."

"What?" she asks in surprise.

"I think I gave Vince all I had," I tell her in a surprising moment of truth that I just now seemed to understand. "I didn't love him enough to give myself to him so freely. He didn't give me enough so I'd want to give him back more."

"Whoa, shit," Elena mutters in a whisper. "You love Walsh?"

I give her a smile. "I think what I feel for him surpasses just love. Our lives are so complicated and have been entwined forever, so what I feel for him is just so much more than the way I loved Vince."

"Girl," Elena says as she blinks her eyes to dispel some tears that has formed. "That is some powerful shit. Making me cry and everything."

I pat her arm and laugh. "Well, things are beyond messed up right now, but I'm hoping that my dreams will turn into reality at some point."

"I have faith they will," she says with a resolute nod of her head. "Now… you are stunning. Go get your man. You two go get your rocks off spectacularly while I go home and eat cookie dough."

Standing up, I reach out and grab Elena for a hard hug. "Thank you for being the best friend imaginable. I don't know what I'd ever do without you."

"Aww… I love you, tootsie," she says as she hugs me back just as hard.

♦

"I CAN'T BELIEVE you recreated the feathers," Walsh says in wonder as we walk hand in hand through The Silo. I take in the scene, note the various people having sex, or just mingling. I smile to myself at the stocks in the room next to the dildo machine, as Walsh had me in there one night.

I've become a complete exhibitionist, getting off now on people watching us together. It's so fucking dirty and liberating at the same time. I'd love to go somewhere else with Walsh and have public sex with him, but I'm terrified of getting arrested so that will probably never happen. I snicker at the thought.

"What's so funny?" Walsh asks as he leads me to the hallway that goes behind the glassed rooms. Walsh reserved the dildo machine for eleven, so it's ready and waiting for us. The only thing different tonight was I didn't wear panties, and only because it was moot. They were coming off as soon as I walked in the door.

"I was just thinking I'd like to have public sex with you somewhere, but I'm afraid of getting busted," I tell him truthfully.

He gives me a deep laugh in return and pulls my hand up to his mouth for a quick kiss. "I'll make it happen, baby."

"Where?" I ask suspiciously.

"Hell, there are any number of hotels here that I can get a room that looks practically into the next building over. We'll go fuck all night up against the window. Plenty of people will see us."

Well, damn… that makes me wet.

Walsh opens the door to our room that holds Micah's amazing invention, and I get even wetter.

"God, Walsh," I whisper to him as he drops my hand and shuts the door. "I think I can actually feel my heartbeat in my clit right now."

He chuckles and steps into me. One hand goes to my neck as he presses his mouth to mine in a deep kiss. The other goes in between my legs as he rubs my clit for research purposes.

"Totally throbbing," he says against my mouth and I laugh back at him. Then he's turning me to the machine and says, "Let's get you saddled up. I've got a raging hard-on, so I want to make you come a few times, fuck your ass, then I want to go back to my apartment and start season three of Sons of Anarchy."

That makes me giggle. I've been introducing Walsh to some of my favorite TV shows as he's never been a guy who just likes to lay around and chill. But that's certainly changing.

For the moment, we ignore the people outside of the glass window. I can sense them pressing in, but Walsh keeps me otherwise preoccupied as he leads me up to the machine. Before he asks me to even straddle it, he brings his hands to my face and kisses me again. This time it's soft and sweet and so contrary to what we're getting ready to do.

"You're amazing, Jorie," he murmurs to me. "There's no one who could ever compare to you."

I smile at him, my heart turning to absolute mush. "I feel the same, Walsh. It's only you."

"Alright then," he says softly and spins me to the machine. "Work yourself down on that cock, baby."

It's for total flare that I pull the stretchy material of my dress up so the curve of my ass is bared to the crowd but the mystery of my pussy stays covered. Walsh wouldn't care if I stripped completely as he has no problem with people looking… just touching.

Walsh holds the dildo for me as I start to work it in. I flex and rotate my hips, taking it into my body an inch at a time. I was so wet at the thought of doing this with Walsh that it slides in easily. When I'm seated to the hilt, Walsh takes the remote control off a small table. I feel his hand at my back and my eyes flutter closed as he turns it on a very low vibration. It doesn't even move up and down, just buzzes within me.

So fucking nice. I lean forward, turn my head, and rest my cheek against the padded incline bench. I open my eyes to look at people watching, and I'm paralyzed with horror as I realize Micah is standing at the back of the crowd with fury in his eyes.

"Oh, fuck," I cry out as I scramble off the dildo.

Walsh is so stunned that he grabs my hips to steady me. "What's wrong, Jor?"

"Micah," I say as tears form in my eyes. "I just saw him at the back of the crowd."

"Impossible," Walsh murmurs, but he looks around The Silo, same as me. We both see him storming out the door at the same time.

I don't hesitate. I pull my dress down and run for the door, Walsh close on my heels.

I can hear the murmur of confused people as they watch us emerge from the back hallway and run for the exit.

We chase after Micah. Although I don't see him anymore, there's no doubt he's on his way out of the club. Walsh and I spend a tense, quiet ride down the elevator as I don't bother trying to hold the tears back. Walsh tries to reach out to me, but I shake my head furiously, too overwhelmed with embarrassment and shame that Micah saw me like that. I feel like I'm going to puke.

When the elevator hits the lobby of the hotel, Walsh bursts out and shoots across the marble floor. He pushes through the doorway, me right behind him, and we come to a stop as we look left and right for my brother. We both locate him down at the end of the block, and we run that way. We come to a stop a few feet away as Micah just stands there, not moving.

Back to us, head down, shoulders slumped.

"Micah," I say in absolute misery.

He turns on us, his face a mask of rage, then he's swinging so hard and fast I can't even cry out a warning. Micah's fist connects with Walsh's jaw, whose head rocks back and he stumbles a few feet. He stays upright, though, and doesn't make a move to retaliate or defend himself.

"You fucking bastard," Micah shouts at him with both fists clenched. "I knew you had something for my sister, you perverted fuck. And you dragged her into this life—"

"No, Micah," I yell at him, but he refuses to look at me. "That's not what happened. It was an accident—"

Micah's head snaps my way and his words are laced

with so much disgust, I flinch. "What? You just fell off that dildo and onto his dick, Jorie? God, don't you haven't any shame?"

Before I know it, Walsh's fist flies out and catches Micah in the jaw. He also rocks back, but doesn't go down.

Beyond enraged, Micah holds his arms out. "Is this the way you want it? Want another crack at me? Take your best shot, Walsh, because then I'm going to stomp your ass into the ground."

Walsh does nothing more than grit out through his teeth, "I don't want to fight you, but I will. And if you ever talk about your sister like that again, they'll be scraping you off the sidewalk when I'm done with you."

"Stop it, both of you," I yell as I walk in between them, holding my hands out. "Please… can we just go talk about this somewhere private?"

I turn to my brother in desperation. "Micah, please… this started off not how you think, and well… this isn't what you think…"

"So I don't think I just saw you in a fucking sex club with Walsh?" he asks me acidly.

"We care about each other," I tell him quietly.

Micah jerks his head toward Walsh. "He cares about nothing but exploiting you."

"That's not true," I say.

"Oh, yeah… then how come he sent me a picture of you while you were on that machine?" Micah asks, and before I can get a chance to explain that, he's continuing to yell at me, "It wasn't too hard to figure out. You were both acting weird at dinner. I caught the subtle little looks you gave each other. Then when I'd heard last night you'd been banging some black-haired, green-eyed girl, well... it wasn't fucking rocket science. I followed you both from The Royale here. And tonight, you're wearing the same goddamn outfit from the night he sent me the photo."

"Micah," I plead with him. "If you will just calm down—"

"Calm down?" Micah screams at me and points at Walsh. "Did you hear me? He sent me a fucking photo of my sister riding a goddamn dildo machine that I created. Do you know he sent that to me knowing I'd get worked up over the hot piece of ass on it? It fucking disgusts me knowing that was you in the photo."

"I'm sorry," I try to explain. "But he didn't know it was me, and I didn't know—"

"You're awful quiet, Walsh," Micah says as he cuts me off and turns his wrath to Walsh. "How come Jorie's the only one trying to plead her case?"

"Brother," Walsh says in a soothing voice, but keeping his distance so as not to be threatening. "I knew this was wrong. We both did. The last thing I wanted to do was lose you as a friend, and so yeah... we were wrong for hiding it from you."

"I'm not your fucking, brother," Micah practically

spits at him. "You should have told me. Instead, you two played out a fucking act right in front of my face this weekend."

"Yes, we did that—" I start to say, but I'm cut off again as he takes a threatening step toward Walsh, who holds his ground.

Then Micah lowers the boom, his voice going deadly quiet with menace. "The worst, Walsh, is that Jorie is as close to a sister as you'll ever have. You fucking helped me change her diapers when she was a baby. It's goddamn sick what you're doing to her."

My stomach plunges and rolls, nausea making me dizzy with the accusation.

"What do you want me to do?" Walsh asks softly.

For the first time, I feel a true rush of fear course through me.

Micah points at me, but looks at Walsh with hateful eyes. "I want you to stay the fuck away from my sister. In fact, stay the fuck away from me, too."

My heart cramps with an immense pain when I see Walsh nod his head in silent agreement.

"No," I start to say, but Micah grabs my arm.

"Come on, Jorie. I'm taking you home."

I jerk free of Micah and turn to Walsh. "Please don't do this. It's out in the open now. We can—"

Walsh's words pierce through me. "Go with Micah, Jorie. It's over."

"No," I say again as I move toward him. He takes a

step back and holds his hands up in a silent statement that he doesn't want me. It infuriates me so greatly, I snap. I literally fucking snap. As tears start free-falling down my face, I scream at Walsh. "You can't do this to me. Not after everything we shared. It's not fair."

Micah comes up behind me and puts his hands on my shoulders, but I'm so pissed at him for making Walsh do this that I jerk free. I take a step toward Walsh and lower myself to utter begging. "Please, Walsh… don't push me away. Don't do this to me."

I can see the pain on his face, but I can also see the deference he's giving Micah for all the sins we just got busted on. He merely whispers, "I'm sorry," and then he walks away.

CHAPTER 21

Walsh

I LOOK AT Jorie's latest text to me—*Please just talk to me*—and I can barely stand to read it. I should block her number, but the thought of doing that tears me up from the inside out.

At least twenty times a day, I consider calling Micah up and telling him to go fuck himself... that there's nothing wrong with me being with Jorie. I want to tell him nothing has ever been more right in my life.

But I don't, because I'm way too deep into my head with misgivings about everything. Micah is so fucking adamant that it's wrong for me to be intimate with Jorie that he's got me questioning my feelings. What if I only wanted to fuck her for the wrongness of it? I'm a kinky son of a bitch who gets off on taboo things. Is it possible that Jorie turns me on because it's wrong?

And what if what Jorie and I have is nothing but sex? That's how it was with Renee. Just fabulous fucking all the time. Now granted, what Jorie and I have together is about a million times more intense and personal than what I had with Renee, but still... what if I'm only addicted to the sex?

More importantly, could I ever look past the sex to the other things that Jorie needs? Family, children, and commitment? I've never wanted to have that with a woman, so what about Jorie is different?

Lastly, and still important to me, is that I need Micah's forgiveness. He can say he isn't all he wants, but he is my brother in every way that matters. Nothing has come between us before, and if I were to tell him to go fuck himself and take his sister for my own, I would never get the forgiveness I want.

No... need.

I need it because what I did was wrong from the beginning. In hindsight, sure... we should have handled it differently, but we didn't, and Micah got tremendously hurt in the process. I've got to have that forgiveness from him or I'll never be able to move on.

I delete Jorie's text like I have the others she sent me over the past five days. At first, she called me. The voice mails were awful to listen to, but I did. I made myself hear her pain and let it score me deep like a thousand paper cuts to my soul.

When Jorie showed up at The Royale as I suspected she would, she caused an understated scene outside the locked door that led to the private elevator. I'd changed the code, and when she couldn't get in, she slid to the floor and cried. My understanding from the direct report I received from Bentley was she sat there for almost half an hour before she finally left.

I also let that cut me deep, the pain in my chest excruciatingly brutal. But I didn't let it sway me. Jorie would eventually move on and find someone who would love her right. That would have a genuine care for her heart. I kept the wall up around me and didn't let her in, knowing that ignoring her pleas was the worst kind of cruelty I could bestow upon her and yet the best favor she could get from me.

I can't give in. If I were to see her... talk to her... fuck, if I were to respond to a single text, I'd give in and tell Micah to go fuck himself.

And I just can't do that.

That would be wrong, too, because he didn't deserve what we did to him.

With a sigh, I roll off my couch and head over to my wet bar. Alcohol has provided some balm to the pain, but I have to get pretty drunk for it to work. Which is fine.

I have no desire to do anything else. The thought of The Wicked Horse repulses me, and I wrote to Jerico that I was canceling my membership. He emailed me back and tried to poke and prod into the issue, but I ignored him.

So I drink, get drunk, sleep, and go to work.

I repeat the process over and over again, and I'm

wondering at what point it starts to get easier.

Five days running now since Micah caught us and demanded I stay away from his sister, and it's just not fucking working.

I switch to the text I sent Micah yesterday. I'd hoped he had time to calm down, so I threw caution to the wind and reached out.

What can I do to fix this between us?

He's not responded to me, and it makes me feel like utter shit. I expect it's how Jorie feels that I'm not responding to her.

I pour myself a vodka on the rocks and take it back to my couch. Listlessly, I put my feet on the coffee table. I rest the glass on my stomach and stare at nothing, knowing I'll drop even deeper into my morose thoughts.

My phone rings and I look down at it slowly. I want it to be Micah telling me everything's all right. I want him to tell me it's okay for me to love Jorie.

Sadly, it's Bentley, and I tense up wondering if Jorie is downstairs.

"Hello," I answer hesitantly.

"Sorry to disturb you, Mr. Brooks," Bentley says in his regal voice that's pretty impressive. "But I have a Miss Elena Sanchez here to see you. She wanted me to advise you that if you don't let her up, she's going to, and I quote, 'go apeshit and cause so much mayhem and destruction, your stock prices will drop'. What would you like me to do?"

I can't fucking help the curve to my lips over her audacity, but truth be told... I expected this at some point.

"Go ahead and let her up, Bentley," I tell him and then push up off the couch. I drain my vodka. By the time I have it refilled, Elena's walking into my living room.

"Want a drink?" I ask her cordially as I turn her way.

"No, I don't want a fucking drink," she snaps at me with fire in her eyes. "I want to talk to you about fixing this shit. Jorie is devastated. She won't get out of bed."

My teeth clench, and my heart pretty much shrivels up into a painful knot deep in my chest.

"Micah's been calling her and she won't talk to him," Elena continues. "I can't get her to eat. She's so depressed and I think... I'm worried she might harm herself."

"What?" I yell at Elena as the glass of vodka falls from my hand and thuds on the carpet. I move toward the elevator. "You think she could hurt herself and you fucking left her alone?"

Elena grabs my arm. "Well, no... Jorie would never do that. But the situation is dire, and I need you to act."

"What the fuck, Elena?" I snarl at her as I jerk my arm away. "Is she okay?"

"Um... well, she won't leave the apartment and she really isn't eating. She's completely heartbroken."

"Do you think she's going to hurt herself?" I enunciate each word slowly and with simmering anger.

"Of course not," Elena admits. "She's not that far in despair, but she is really, really in the pits. You need to do something."

"That is not fucking cool to throw that shit at me," I growl as I push past her and pick up my empty vodka glass. I ignore the soaked spot on the rug and pour another.

"You're just going to sit here and get drunk while Jorie is in pain?" Elena asks from behind me.

"Jorie will move on," I mutter.

"No, Walsh… she won't. You were it for her. There is nothing else."

I didn't think that shriveled knot in my chest could hurt worse, but it does. I take a huge swallow of vodka and let it warm me from within.

"Don't you love her?" Elena asks me quietly.

I don't answer out loud, but inside, it's a resounding yes. I've loved her for decades and then some. I'll continue to love her decades into the future.

"Do you?" Elena presses.

"It's complicated," is all I'll admit to, as I walk up to the windows looking out over Vegas.

"Fuck yeah, it's complicated," she proclaims with exasperation. "But complicated doesn't mean unfixable."

"Micah has to cool down first," I say distractedly. "I've got to fix it with him first."

"No," Elena says angrily. She marches up to me,

positioning herself between me and the windows with a hard glare. "You have to fix it with Jorie right now. She's the most important."

I know she's right about this but, sadly, I can only believe that really fixing this means I give her up. Fixing this means I sit down with her face to face, apologize to her and let her rant at me. I sit through begging and pleading and declarations of love, and when that's all over, I have to tell her we can't go on.

At least, I think that's how it has to be fixed.

Fuck… I don't know what needs to be done except that alcohol lets me avoid the hard answers. So, I take another solid slug.

After I swallow, I turn the tables on Elena. "Let me ask you a question, and you answer me honestly as the person who probably knows Jorie best in this world."

"Okay," she says hesitantly.

"What if I told you right now that I couldn't give Jorie what she really wanted? Marriage, children, a home to share with me. Would you still want me to try or let her move on?"

Elena swallows hard, and I can see it's a bitter pill by the look on her face when she admits, "I'd want her to move on. Those things are too important to her."

"You have your answer then," I tell her softly. "I can't give her those things."

This, of course, is a lie. I could easily give her those things because I love her. But with shit so fucked up with her brother, it does no good to even consider those possibilities.

Elena just stares at me a moment, and then says, "Let me ask you a question, and then I want an honest answer from a man who has seen all the beauty Jorie brings to life... how bleak is your life without her right now, and do you think it will get any better as you 'move on'?"

Jesus... the worst question of all because it forces me to put *me* as a priority, and I just can't. I've fucked up so many things, hurt people I care about deeply, and if I answer this question honestly, that means I have to stand up and take what I want.

I'd have to be a selfish fuck to do that right now.

I lie to Elena because I've found I'm very good at it lately.

I tell her what she needs to hear to let this go, and hopefully to help Jorie move toward a happy existence without me. "I believe it will get better. Every day that goes by, I'm getting a little more peace about this."

Elena's head tilts as she takes this in. I hold my eyes locked to hers and don't blink. I'm absolutely bluffing, but I have an amazing poker face.

Finally, I see sadness fill her expression and her shoulders sag. "Well, okay then. Maybe Jorie needs to move on."

I grit my teeth hard so I don't admit to my lie, and just nod at Elena. She turns and walks out of my apartment without another word.

Grabbing my vodka, I head back to my couch, resume my position before Elena interrupted my brooding, and call Micah out of desperation. Not surprised when I get his voice mail.

At the tone, I leave him a message. "Micah... please know I'm so sorry for lying to you about Jorie. I know you think it's wrong for me to be with her, but she's not my sister. She's someone I care about... deeply. What you saw in the club... that's not all there is to us. It's how it started... really by accident. It was a masquerade event, and we didn't recognize each other. I swear to fucking God, we didn't know. But when I did—"

Beep.

"Fuck," I yell out to my empty apartment as I stab Micah's phone number again so it rings.

I continue my message when I hear the tone. "When I realized it was Jorie, I couldn't contain what I was feeling. I guess that night I got drunk and rambled on about her to you... well, I think deep down, I've always wanted her. I'm sorry, brother... and you are my brother. I hope you remember that. Please, please call me so we can talk this through. I want—"

Beep.

I curse and throw my phone across the room. It hits the wet bar and I hope the goddamn thing is broken. Otherwise, I'd be tempted to call Jorie next.

CHAPTER 22

Jorie

"HEY... YOU DOING okay?" Elena asks me as she pops her head into my room.

I look up from my computer and give her a forced smile, but there's some truth in it because I'm happy to see her. She always brightens my day.

"Yeah... sure," I tell her as I nod down to my computer. "Checking out some more places to apply."

"Where?" she asks sadly, because she knows I'm talking about far away.

"Bigger cities... New York, Boston, Pittsburgh... maybe Miami, but not sure I can handle that humid heat," I tell her as my throat threatens to close at the thought of moving so far away.

But I think it's the best thing.

Ironically, I was offered the position I'd applied for here in Henderson the day after Micah found out about me and Walsh. I was too distraught to even reply to them, and after a few days, I'm sure they got the hint I wasn't interested.

And I wasn't.

I was only interested in leaving Nevada.

"Those are all East Coast," Elena states the obvious.

"I know," I say glumly. "I thought about Europe, but figured that was a little too far away from you."

She smiles and comes to sit on the edge of my bed. I'm propped up against the headboard and move my computer to the mattress beside me.

"Do you think," I start off hesitantly, and I can see she knows what's coming by the empathetic look on her face, "that if he knew I was leaving, that would spur him to do something?"

Elena's expression turns even more sad, and she reaches out to take my hand. "I went to see him."

"When?" I ask in shocked surprise, my hand clutching hers harder.

"A few days ago," she says and just stares at me.

I stare right back at her.

Finally, with a tiny wince, she says, "You need to move on, Jorie. It's not going to happen."

God, my chest feels like it's going to cave in the pain hits me so hard. I thought after over a week without Walsh, it would get easier to handle, but this is just as devastating to hear than when he walked away from me.

Immensely more heartbreaking than every text or call he ignored. Because after every one of them, I still had hope. I still had belief he'd come around.

But Elena's seen him. She's talked to him.

She's telling me the truth. Walsh is never coming for me.

"God," I whisper as I press the palm of my hand into my chest and tears fill my eyes. "Why does this hurt so much?"

"Because you love him," she says softly. I note she doesn't tell me that he loves me. Clearly, she didn't get that from her meeting with him.

I nod in understanding and when I blink, the tears fall.

"Oh, Jorie," she says in shared misery and opens her arms up. I lean forward and fall into them, putting my head on her shoulder. Staring at my bedroom wall made blurry by the tears falling heavy, I let her hold me.

Finally, I dry up and lift my head. She jumps up from the bed, runs to the bathroom, and returns with a roll of toilet paper. I take off several sheets and dry my face.

The doorbell rings to the apartment and just ten minutes ago, I would have been exhilarated at the thought it was Walsh coming to beg for me back. But I trust Elena and if she told me I need to move on, then that's not him.

I sit back against the headboard and pull my computer back onto my lap.

"I'll go get that," she says and then asks, "want to go out tonight for dinner? Tacos and tequila?"

I give her a watery smile. "Sure."

Elena leaves, pulling my bedroom door shut behind me. I look back to the website for The Miami Herald, trying to navigate to a section that contains contact information for job applications.

A soft knock on my door causes my head to snap up, and then I'm utterly floored when I see Vince standing there with just his head pushing through. "Can I come in?"

"Um... yeah," I say in bewilderment. "But what are you doing here?"

Vince walks in and shuts the door. He looks at me silently a moment, keenly taking in my red eyes and blotchy skin before he says, "I was worried about you. You haven't been responding to me this past week. Not even a 'go to hell, Vince'."

I give him a small smile and move over so he can come sit on the edge of the bed. He takes a seat with casual ease, and I take a second to appreciate how handsome my husband is. Sandy-blond hair worn in a business cut, face always cleanly shaven. He's wearing my favorite cologne and dressed casually in shorts and a polo shirt.

"You didn't have to come here," I tell him.

"You're clearly having a tough time," he returns softly. "And you're my wife. I love you. Of course I had to come and check on you, even if I'm part of that hard time."

"Vince—"

"Is your heart broken, Jorie?" he asks me simply.

I nod, unable to voice the words because my throat is clogged. The tears in my eyes speak volumes and Vince's face turns sad and empathetic all at once.

"It's not me who broke your heart though?" he asks.

I blink hard, wipe my face with more toilet paper, and give a little cough. "You did break my heart. But I fell for someone, and it got broken again."

I can tell he's being careful with his words and he's genuinely curious, if not a little hurt when he asks, "Not to doubt your feelings, but how did you fall for someone that fast? In just a matter of weeks."

"It's Walsh." It takes him a moment to understand who I mean.

"Micah's friend?" he asks. They've never met, but he's heard Micah talk about him plenty and I've talked about him a little bit over our years of marriage.

I nod again. "I didn't expect it to happen. Wasn't looking for it, but…"

"But why wouldn't you?" he asks with some self-recrimination. "I gave you every reason to."

"It's okay," I say candidly. "I've been doing a lot of reflection, and I don't think I was the wife you needed me to be."

"Not true," he says immediately. "I was a selfish asshole who got stuck on myself. I saw I wasn't the husband you needed. I boiled it down to sex, and honestly, I'm selfish in bed, too. I think I took and didn't give enough."

I shrug. "I don't have it all figured out. But maybe we're both right."

There's a heavy moment of silence, and Vince pushes off the bed. He paces around the small room, looking at nothing really because I have nothing of me in here. This was only ever supposed to be temporary for me.

Finally, he turns around and says, "I've been reflecting, too."

I tilt my head, oddly at ease with my husband for some reason. He's being so transparent, and I've never seen that before.

"I don't think I had my priorities right in life," he says hesitantly. "When I asked you to leave, I had put myself at the top of the totem pole. Right below that was my job, and Jorie… it embarrasses the fuck out of me to admit this, but I'm not even sure you were next. I don't think there was anything else after that, and I'm just so sorry I failed you in that respect."

Tears spring into my eyes again. I'm completely blown away by his admission. In our entire marriage, Vince has never taken responsibility for his flaws. He's refused to believe he's anything less than perfect.

"Thank you for saying that," I say quietly.

He nods and comes back to the bed, sitting beside me. When he takes my hand, I let him, because it feels safe and secure. "I know I'm not the cause of your current heartbreak, but if you let me… I'd like to help you fix it."

My eyebrows draw inward. "What do you mean?"

"I mean, come back home with me," he says with earnest determination. "Give me another chance. Let me try to fix what I broke. I'll go to counseling if that will help, but I'm not ready to throw away eight years with you so easily."

I stare at him with astonishment. I know this man very well, and I've never seen him show such genuine vulnerability before. It's so contrary to the man I know, I'm not sure I can trust it. Still, we have eight years together, and I need to hear him out.

"Vince… you understand I'm broken because I love another man," I say softly, knowing that's going to hurt.

He winces but nods. "I get that. But you loved me once, didn't you?"

"Very much," I admit.

"Then come home with me and let me see if I can get that back. I'll take it slow if you want. You set the pace. But come with me and let me take care of you the way you deserve. If nothing else, it will give you a safe place away from bad memories. If you do nothing more than just heal, it will make me feel good to help you do that."

The timing of Vince's visit couldn't be better. The timing couldn't be worse. He's caught me at the lowest point of my life, and he offers me a life raft. I did love

Vince very much. I love Walsh so much more.

But of the two loves of my life, there's only one standing before me offering to help heal my broken heart.

I give Vince's hand a squeeze. "It's a nice offer for a girl like me."

"But?"

"But even if you and I fix everything that you broke by the way you asked me to leave, there's still a fundamental difference between us."

Vince looks genuinely perplexed. "What's that?"

"Children," I say simply.

"Children?" he repeats, as if he doesn't understand the concept.

"You don't want them," I remind him.

"Who said I don't want them?" he returns, and my jaw just drops open.

"Vince," I say with disbelief. "After I miscarried, you were relieved because you weren't ready. And you've always disliked kids. Whenever we're around other kids, you're always complaining about them."

Understanding dawns like the sunlight of a new day on Vince's face, but then his look turns a bit reproachful. "Jorie… you and I haven't really had a serious discussion about this, but let's talk about it now. I wasn't relieved when you miscarried. I was saddened, but I'll admit I was scared shitless to have kids at that point in my life. I wasn't ready to be a parent. I wanted to be a husband first, and figured kids would come later. Much, much later. And yes, I've complained about other kids because those other kids have been assholes. I would hope we wouldn't raise an asshole."

I'm floored again by what he's telling me. "But I was so sure…"

"We've never talked about it, have we?" he asks.

"Well, no."

"Then don't assume," he chides.

"So you want kids?" I ask, because I'm just not believing this.

His words are careful and measured. "I can't say it's at the top of my agenda, but I figured I'd have kids someday. It's the circle of life, right?"

"But do you want kids with me?" I press him. "You can barely stomach having sex with me—"

"That's not true," he interrupts harshly and brings a hand up to hold my jaw so I don't turn my gaze. "I said that to push you away. Things may have gotten a little dull in our bed, but don't think it was just you. It was me, too. Baby… I thought the grass was greener, and yeah… I pushed you away to try it. And it's not greener. It was awful without you, and I figure… sex should be a fucking easy problem to fix, right?"

God, the thought of having sex with Vince feels wrong to me in every way. Not because it couldn't be good, but because my heart is with someone else. Even if I were to give my marriage a shot, I'm not sure I can give him that part of myself.

"Vince… when I tell you I'm in love with another man, it means not just soul, but body."

Unmitigated pain fills Vince's eyes, and that hurts me. I don't like hurting anyone.

But he nods and with the patience of a saint, he says, "I'll wait for you to give that to me then. Come home with me, and there will be no expectations on my part for anything. All you need to do is let me help you forget about this heartbreak. Let's give our marriage a shot."

My eyes slide over and look at my computer where I've been desperately trying to escape my pain by moving across the country. It's not something I really wanted, but I figured running far away and starting fresh would help.

But maybe all I need to do is run to Los Angeles, where I could be back in comfortable surroundings with a man who seems to be willing to let me figure things out at my own pace. I'm so fucking tired and drained, I'm not sure how I can say no to his offer.

I look back to him and take in the genuine desire on his face to make things right with us. With a squeeze to his hand, I say, "I can't promise you anything. I'm not even sure I have the strength to try. But as long as you know I'm all kinds of fucked up in the head and don't know what I'm doing or what I even want anymore, then I'll accept. Just know… if I can't move past Walsh, I'll be honest with you."

"That's all I can ask, Jorie," Vince tells me, and then he leans forward and brushes a chaste kiss on my lips.

I'm not going to lie.

It feels good.

CHAPTER 23

Walsh

"ANOTHER?" THE BARTENDER asks me as I sit huddled over the glass I'd just drained.

I push it toward him with two fingers. "Sure."

I stare at the bar and listen to the sounds of The Silo. Skin slapping, moans, and orgasmic cries. I feel nothing, and I'm not sure how pathetic it makes me by sitting here.

This is the third night in a row I've come to The Wicked Horse. All three nights I've sat at the bar in The Silo.

Not because I'm looking to get laid, but because I can't sit in my apartment anymore. I can't be alone with my misery, so I come here.

Who knows, maybe one day I'll get my hard-on back and take advantage, but it's not tonight.

A new drink gets slid toward me, and I push some money back to the bartender. "Keep the change."

"Thanks, man," he says. You would think I'd get

more than that since I've given him a twenty for each drink so far and told him to keep the change, but whatever.

I'm sure Jerico thinks I'm equally pathetic because I renewed my membership but have done nothing but sit here and drink. I'm paying exorbitant money to have access to a bar in a sex club where I'm not having sex but rather castigating myself.

Jesus, I'm a mess.

Someone sits down beside me, and it only makes me huddle closer to my drink. I don't want conversation. I don't want to fuck.

I want to drink, think about Jorie, and be left alone.

"I'll have a scotch," the person says, and I turn in astonishment to see Micah sitting there.

I take a moment to study him. Bland expression, casual posture. Not here to kick my ass.

Pity.

I turn away from him without a word. Picking up my drink, I take a small sip.

"Not happy to find you here," Micah says. There's no anger in his voice. Just disappointment.

I don't give a fuck, either.

"Don't worry," I say dryly. "I haven't done anything. I'm still pining for your sister, after all."

"You're in a sex club, pining for my sister?" Micah asks in disbelief, and there's a little bit of anger. I find I like it because this douche has ignored me for over two weeks now. "That pisses me off."

Still don't give a fuck.

I shrug as I shoot him a short glance, then turn back to my brooding posture. "What can I say? This is where we first came together, and where we broke up. I'm nostalgic that way."

"Christ," Micah mutters, and I watch from my peripheral vision as the bartender hands him his drink. He knocks it back and slides the empty glass away. "Give me another, and another for him, too."

"Appreciate it," I say glibly.

I ignore Micah and sip at my drink, knowing I have another waiting for me.

"Was Jorie just sex to you?" Micah asks out of the blue, and mission accomplished… he gets an immediate rise out of me.

I twist my neck to look at him and grit out. "If you listened to my fucking voice mails, you'd know that's not true."

"And yet, here you sit in a sex club," he says with a sneer.

"True," I tell him nonchalantly, as I turn back to my drink. "But without a hard-on."

"Not tempted in any way?" he presses, and my anger explodes.

I turn my entire body on the stool and lean aggressively toward him. "What the fuck do you want, Micah? Because you made it clear how you feel about Jorie and me, and I don't fucking feel like hearing more shit about it. I did what you asked. I stayed away from your sister. Now you can stay the fuck away from me, and it's all good. Everybody's happy."

Micah just blinks at me. I wait a moment to make sure he understands me, and then I turn back to my drink.

"Jorie's not happy," Micah says softly.

I snort and bob my head. "No shit, Dick Tracy."

"You're not happy," he says.

I don't respond. That's evident.

"I'm not happy."

"Don't give a fuck about that one," I mutter.

This so called best friend sitting beside me made me give up the one thing in life I loved, but didn't give me the common decency to talk it through.

Micah leaves me alone for a few minutes, and I just start to relax again in my buzzed misery when he says, "She went back to L.A. She's back with Vince."

A wave of despair hits me, making it clear I could feel worse than I did two seconds ago. This is followed by a wave of fury so powerful, I feel like I could kill Micah because this now rests squarely on his fucking shoulders.

To spare him my rage, I merely pick up my money and push from the barstool. Without a word and figuring this is the last time I'll ever see Micah, I turn my back on him and mutter, "I'm out of here."

Shoving my money down into my pocket, I head

toward the door.

"Walsh," Micah calls.

I ignore him and make my way out of The Silo. Down the hall to the Social Room, and down the elevator and out of The Onyx Casino. It was a mistake coming here as there's nothing really left here for me.

The distance from Micah does nothing to cool my anger. How dare he fucking show up in my life and act concerned about everyone's happiness? How dare he fucking throw at me that she's with Vince, because all that means to me is it's too late with Jorie?

Fucking dude's got balls. I should have knocked the bastard out.

"Walsh."

I start walking aimlessly down the street. Turning to look over my shoulders, I see him hurrying after me.

I ignore him, but when his hand lands on my shoulder, the fury erupts.

I turn and throw a roundhouse punch that connects so solidly, he goes careening to the wall of The Onyx. He starts to sag, and I have a moment of pure vindication.

Turning my back on him, I start walking away, but he's not finished.

"Walsh… you have to go after her," Micah calls out. By the wet sound of his words, I know his mouth is filled with blood. That makes me feel good.

"Walsh," Micah calls again, and it's in pure desperation. I falter in my steps. "She loves you still. Not Vince.

Please don't throw her away because I was a fucking douche about this."

My feet plant and refuse to take another step. I turn back to look at him hesitantly. He's leaning against the wall with blood streaming from the corner of his mouth.

Yeah… that still makes me feel good.

But I walk the few steps back to him and say, "Talk."

Micah stands up a little straighter, spits blood out of his mouth, and then wipes it on the sleeve of his shirt. "She loves you, Walsh."

"Tell me something I don't know," I growl at him. Because that's just a painful reminder of what I don't have.

"She doesn't love Vince," he says urgently. "She's only with him because she was so lost, she latched onto the first security that presented itself."

"She told you that?" I ask him.

His eyes cut away guiltily, then back to me. "Not exactly."

"What does that mean?" I snap, running out of patience.

"She's not talking to me. Hasn't since that night."

"Then are you making this shit up about Vince?" I ask in disbelief at the levels he'd sink.

Micah shakes his head. "No. She sent me a single text that just said she was moving back to L.A. with Vince, and she was going to try to figure out what she wanted."

"Nothing about that text says she doesn't love him or

that she wants to be with me," I tell him pointedly, and I have another intense desire to punch him again.

"But it does," he insists. "She said she wanted to figure out what she wanted. Which means she doesn't necessarily want Vince, but you."

I roll my eyes at him and turn to walk away. "You'll have to do better than that."

"Walsh… you both love each other. Don't fucking walk away from that."

Rage flows through me again, and I spin on Micah. His hands come up protectively, but I don't physically strike out. Instead, I yell at him, "How do you know that, Micah? You wouldn't fucking listen to us that night, so tell me how you know shit about what's between your sister and me, you motherfucking, cocksucking asshole."

"Okay, I deserve that," he says hastily. Suddenly, all my anger just dies.

I feel a hundred years old, beaten and broken, so I ask him again, "How do you know?"

"Because I saw Jorie pleading with you that night to not leave her," he says quietly. "I heard the pain in her voice. I saw the heartbreak on her face when you walked away."

"*You* made me walk away from her," I accuse.

"Yes," he agrees readily. "I was so fucking mired in my own anger that I couldn't see anything else. But I see it now, Walsh. She loves you. Don't sit here and tell me you don't love her back, because that would be a fucking lie."

I don't respond, but my jaw clenches tight as I listen.

"You love me, too," Micah adds.

Once again, I want to punch him.

"I despise you," I mutter.

"No… you love me. You walked away from my sister because I asked you to, and you did that because you love me."

"But not anymore," I growl at him, but the last of my anger ebbs away, and I notice with strange awareness there's a flicker of hope within me. "I still want to kick your ass."

"If that will make you feel better," Micah says as he throws his arms out wide. "I'll do anything to help make this right. But Walsh… I've been two weeks without my best friend and my sister, and it's killing me. I miss you both so much, and it's absolutely just killing me that you two are in pain because of my selfishness. You've got to let me back in, and you've got to get Jorie back."

"Start by telling me everything you know about her and Vince getting back together," I tell him as I start walking toward The Royale. It's several blocks away, but the air is helping to clear my head.

Micah rushes to catch up with me. "I talked to Elena before I flew out here today. She said Vince showed up at the apartment four days ago and convinced Jorie to come back with him."

"What's his agenda?" I ask, so I can figure out how to shut it down fast.

"I don't think he has one," Micah says dejectedly. "Elena felt he was being genuine and really wants to work things out with her, but he promised he'd give her space to figure things out first."

"Fuck," I mutter. That presents a huge problem. First, Jorie is married to this dude, and I swore I wouldn't stand in the way if she wanted to save her marriage. I have to decide if I'm being selfish by trying to impede that.

"He told her he wants kids," Micah adds.

"Fuck, fuck, fuck," I curse under my breath.

Micah's hand on my arm stops me in my tracks, and I turn to look at him. His eyes are solemn when he asks, "Do you want children with her? Marriage? Because if you don't, then let them be. Let Jorie figure it out on her own."

"I want everything with your sister. If she'll have me, I want to give her everything she wants and then more on top of that. I'm thinking three, maybe four kids, but we'd have to talk about that. A house in the suburbs. Fuck, I want a white picket fence with her and a golden retriever named Scout or some shit like that."

Micah's lips peel back into a bloody grin, which seems completely macabre, but it makes me smile back at him.

His smile dies a little. "I'm really sorry, Walsh. I

should have given you the benefit of the doubt. I should have never been wigged out by this in the first place. It was a huge mistake, and I've caused a lot of hurt that I'm asking you to fix for me."

There's no hesitation when my arm shoots around his neck, and I pull him to me for an awkward bro hug with a huge back slap.

Yes, I hope it hurts a little.

When I release him, I say, "Let's go get me packed up. I've got a flight to catch to L.A. in the morning."

CHAPTER 24

Jorie

I RINSE MY coffee cup out and put it in the dishwasher. The counters are pristine and wiped off. Vince and I bought this—our second house—about four years ago after we'd saved up money. I thought it was my dream home, but I'm realizing that real dreams having nothing to do with granite countertops and Viking appliances.

Still, I made this house into a home, and I smile fondly at all my touches. Buttercup-yellow paint in the kitchen, cream suede couches in the spacious living room, and elegant lamps in the bedroom. All little things I'd picked out that said, "Jorie was here".

I walk through to the master bathroom and brush my teeth. Love my coffee, but hate the sour aftertaste.

Vince graciously gave me the master suite when I came home with him. I can't say he offered it altruistically, because I could see he had immediate hope I'd share the bed with him. I knew this because that first evening, he'd pulled me into his arms and tried to kiss me.

The turning of my head away from his mouth was an indication I clearly was not ready for that.

That's when he graciously told me I should take the master suite, and he would stay in one of the upstairs bedrooms until I was ready to cross that bridge.

I must say, outside of that, life back here with Vince has been a pleasant surprise. While we may not be intimate, we've lapsed into a comfortable existence with one another. I've found myself smiling, and... that's solely due to Vince. He's been charming, amusing, and he's really been listening to me when we've talked. I can tell he's trying his hardest to show me that he wants this to work, and he's even being patient by letting me set the pace of things. So far, all I can give him is friendship.

This hurts my heart, because I'm not sure if I can do anything more than that. I'm still unbelievably incapacitated by the hurt of losing Walsh, and it's still not getting any better. If anything, I've layered anger over the top of the pain, because after I grieved, I had to move on to the other stages, right?

And I'm fine in the anger stage for now.

I'm pissed as hell at my brother and Walsh.

Micah for not giving us a chance to explain and driving Walsh away from me.

And Walsh... well, I'm pissed he let Micah drive him away. I don't like forcing someone to choose, but in this case, and as I feed on some of my bitterness, I know he made a mistake in not picking me over Micah. If he'd done that, he could have still had me, and we would have worked on Micah together. I know my brother; he would have come around eventually.

But Walsh was too fucking scared or cowardly or I don't know what, but he never considered that option in the first place.

Asshole.

God, I love him, but I want to hate him.

My phone rings, and I realize I left it back in the kitchen. I rush through the house, see Vince's number, and answer it cheerily. "Hey you."

"Hey, Jorie," he says affectionately, and I have to admit… that sounds really nice to my soul.

"What's up?" I ask him as I lean over the kitchen island.

"My lunch appointment got canceled, and I wanted to know if I could take you out. Want to meet me at Cristo's in about forty-five minutes?"

I laugh. "You know I can't pass up their Reuben."

"Exactly," he says as a husband who knows Cristo's makes my favorite sandwich in the world, and I'm totally addicted to the rye bread they use.

"Okay, see you then," I say.

"See you then," he says back, and then adds on, "Love you."

Simple words that got thrown about so casually in our marriage. Every phone call ended with that, or as he was rushing out the door to work, he'd throw "Love you," out to me. I'd always call back, "Love you too".

This time, I don't because it doesn't come to me easily. My lips are practically glued shut. Instead, I just say, "I'll see you soon."

"Okay," he says, and I can hear the disappointment in his voice. "See you soon."

Forty-five minutes doesn't give me much time, especially because I want to stop by the post office and mail a package to Elena. I found the most beautiful scarf while out shopping yesterday, and I knew she'd love it.

I rush back to my room, checking my hair and makeup. I put a little bit of cherry Chapstick on and grab my purse to head out.

When I open the door, I'm brought to a complete halt by someone standing there.

A big hulking someone actually, and it takes several beats of my heart before I can process it's Walsh with his finger outstretched toward my doorbell.

"What are you doing here?" I'm able to finally push out around the emotion clogging my throat.

"I'm here to bring you back to Vegas with me," he says confidently, and while I'll admit a thrill of adrenaline spikes through me at that alpha proclamation, all my hurt and anger throw up a huge wall.

"Not interested," I say as I start to push past him. "And I'm running late. I've got to meet Vince for lunch."

"Yeah, that's not going to work for me," Walsh says as his palm goes to my chest and he gently pushes me back inside. He follows me in, shuts the door, and turns the lock. "You're going to have to be late."

"Walsh," I sputter, but then his mouth is on mine and he's kissing me like I've never been kissed before.

His hands deep in my hair, fingers curled to grip it tight. He shoves his tongue into my mouth, and he bends me almost backward as he claims me.

When he pulls his lips from mine, he demands in a snarling way that tells me the answer is very important, "Have you fucked him?"

I shake my head no, and then I go dizzy when he pulls me up, spins me to the door, and pushes me back into it. Words of protest are stuck deep within me when Walsh goes to his knees, puts his hands up my sundress, and roughly drags my panties down my legs. I feel the cool air hit me there, and it feels cooler than it should because I'm wet.

Fuck.

Lifting each one of my legs in turn, Walsh pulls my panties free without so much as a protest from me. Then he's pushing my dress up, hauling a single leg over his shoulder, and burying his face in my pussy. He gives out a groan and then inhales deeply, a move that's so fucking erotic I almost collapse. But then my leg locks straight as his tongue circles my clit and his fingers slip inside me.

I bring my hands to Walsh's head, and I try to push him off with a feeble protest that's a bit of a lie, but he doesn't need to know that. "Walsh, please stop. I'm with

Vince—"

His head pulls back, and he glares up at me. "Say his fucking name again while I'm tongue fucking you and you're not going to like what I do."

Our eyes stay locked, and I can't say anything. I want to just say "Vince" to see what Walsh would do, because I bet it would involve him slapping my pussy, but I don't poke the bear. He waits a moment more for me to tell him to stop. When I don't, he dives back in. He licks and sucks. Fucks me with his fingers. He waits until I'm on the edge of an orgasm, and then he pulls his lips away to look up at me and say things like, "God, I missed this" and "This is my pussy" and "You better fucking scream my name when you come, Jorie."

My orgasm starts to brew hard again and my whimpering lets Walsh know I'm close. He starts to pull away from me, the torturous bastard, but I'm having none of it. I grip his hair hard, flex my hips, and rub myself hard against his mouth. I can feel his lips peel back into an amused grin, and he gives a tiny nip to my clit.

I explode viciously, screaming out his name like he told me to.

I'm still shuddering with tiny micro bursts of pleasure when he surges up and whips his cock out of his pants so fast I don't even have time to admire it. He's got me in his arms, back slammed into the door, and he's driving into me so deeply, I feel another climax start.

Walsh is so lost inside of me, he grunts like an animal every time he thrusts in. I claw at his shoulders and rotate my hips, trying to get him deeper. I moan and whimper and pant, begging him for more.

He starts to fuck me so hard, the door starts rattling.

Walsh buries his face into my neck, and his mouth is on me. He gives me a sharp bite before he mutters, "Going to fuck your ass next."

So wrong. So sexy.

The thought of him doing that to me, in my marital home, makes me explode again.

So fucking wrong, but I scream out his name again.

A noise penetrates the fog of lust... a clear squeak that seems to come from the door behind me. Then the slap of mail hitting the wooden foyer floor shocks me silly.

Walsh's hips slow down, and we both look at the mail the mailman just pushed through the slot.

While Walsh was telling me he was going to fuck my ass, and then while I screamed as I orgasmed.

We lock eyes, his cock now gently plunging into me but never stopping.

Then we both burst out laughing. I drop my forehead on his shoulder, and laugh while Walsh continues to grind into me. But the laughs give way to chuckles, which gives way to more panting as Walsh starts going faster again.

His breathing is labored, his cock batters me, and all I can do is hang on for the ride, knowing I'm going to have to deal with the fallout later.

Walsh suddenly plants deep, and I look for the signs of his orgasm. But his eyes don't close, instead locking on to me. He groans out his release while he says, "I fucking miss you, Jorie."

Then he crashes his mouth on mine again. My hands go back to his hair, and I hold him tight to me as we make out while he comes down off his orgasm.

When he finally goes still inside me, he puts his forehead against mine and murmurs, "I love you, Jorie."

Every cell in my body seems to quiet over his words before pure joy bursts out of each one. The feeling is so climactic, I start to cry.

"Shh," he says as he pulls back to look at me. "It's okay."

I shake my head. "It's not."

Walsh's lips press tight, but he nods some sort of understanding to me. I'm immediately terrified he'll give up, but before I can say a word, he lowers me to the floor.

Before he tucks himself into his pants, he's immediately kneeling before me. He takes my panties and has me step into them. After he pulls them up my legs, he comes to a standing position before me as he adjusts the elastic waistband and pulls my dress down.

"You have lunch plans with him?" he asks as he takes care of himself and zips back up.

"Yes."

"Go meet him," he says quietly. "Then you and I are talking after."

I glance at my watch and curse. "Shit. I'm going to be late. I've got to go get a shower."

"Uh-uh," Walsh says as his palm presses me into the door. "You go eat lunch with him with my cum inside you. Let it keep your panties soaked the entire time so you don't forget about me."

Jesus… my eyes glaze over from the lust his words provoke. He gives me a knowing smile and kisses the corner of my mouth.

"I'm going to go get a hotel close by," he says when he pulls back. "I'll text you the information. Come see me after you finish lunch."

"Walsh," I say with uncertainty. "This isn't right."

"Wrong," he says gruffly. "Everything's been right between us from the moment I walked into that hotel bathroom and saw you bleeding. I'm not giving you up. If I have to compete with Vince, so be it. But I tell you right now, Jorie… if you come to my hotel after lunch, we're going to fuck again before we talk. My balls have two weeks of misery to overcome."

I can't help it. I snicker over that, getting a pinch to my ass in return.

With that, I immediately start to fret over what I need to say to Vince.

♦

VINCE ALREADY HAS a table when I arrive at Cristo's, and I'm relieved it sits in a relatively private corner. He stands when I approach and gives me a kiss on my cheek.

I choose the chair that sits adjacent to him for more private conversation. The moment we sit, I tell him the truth. "Walsh came to see me a bit ago."

Vince freezes in place, his napkin halfway to his lap as he watches me with a stunned expression.

"We had sex," I add softly, hating to hurt him but knowing I can't keep that secret. He deserves full honesty.

The air comes out of Vince so forcefully, it's like he got punched in the chest. "You had sex with him? In our house?"

I nod guiltily. "I'm sorry. It's just... what Walsh and I have is very physical. It's very different from what you and I had."

"And you love him?" he asks glumly.

"Yes," I say without hesitation. "But I also love you, and you're my husband."

He blinks at me in surprise, and hope filters into his gaze.

"I truly don't know what I want," I tell him truthfully. "But part of me feels like I owe you a shot or something because you really came through for me, Vince."

"What kind of shot?" he asks.

"I don't know. I'm going to talk to Walsh again after

lunch, but I'm going to tell him to leave. And then you and I need to really talk. I need to tell you everything about what I've been doing the last few weeks, and I need to tell you all about Walsh. There's so much you need to know about our past together."

"Are you going to have sex with him again when you go see him?" Vince asks with a tinge of anger.

"I'm not sure," I tell him, and that's the truth.

"Are you going to have sex with me?" he asks.

"I don't know," I also tell him truthfully. "I want us to talk first. But if this is too much for you to handle, I would understand."

Vince ponders this. He doesn't like the situation, and that's because he has no control. But I can't help it. I've got to make sure about what I'm doing. I love Walsh with all my heart, but he abandoned me. I loved Vince with all my heart, and I still love him with a part of my heart, but he pushed me away.

It's time I figured out what I really want, and I need to be fine with the knowledge that the answer might be that I don't choose either one of them.

"I don't like it," Vince finally says. "But fine… go see him. If you choose to stay in the marriage, I want you to have every opportunity to make sure he's not the guy and I am."

CHAPTER 25

Walsh

It's embarrassing how fast I came fucking Jorie up against that door. Two weeks without her and the knowledge I was claiming her in her husband's home, the one who had the fucking gall to tell her she was bad in bed, made me come fast and hard.

It took the edge off but not nearly enough.

I'm pretty sure I'll attack her the minute she walks in the door, and that should be very soon. She texted me a bit ago to say she was on her way, and I've had a hard-on since then.

I've also been filled with a low-boiling turmoil. Jorie didn't push me away in her house. She let me have her and screamed my name twice with love.

Not orgasm, but love.

I heard it, and so did she.

And then she told me she was with Vince. Christ, that fucking cut. She then told me that what we did wasn't right, and that cut me further. I must face the very real possibility that I've lost her to a man who pulled through for her when she needed it. I don't know the guy personally, can't fucking stand what I do know, yet he did Jorie a solid. He eased her pain for a few days by just being there, and that causes my conscience to tingle a little with wariness.

The knock on the door has me rolling off the bed and trying to adjust my erection away from my zipper as I stand. When I open the door, I want nothing more than to grab her, jerk her into the room, and strip her naked. But the minute I see the look in her eyes, I can't do anything but open my arms to her.

She walks straight into them and starts sobbing. I don't know the why of her tears or how to even fix them, so the only thing I can do is let her get them out.

I sweep her up into my arms and take her to the bed. Taking her down with me, I pull her in close, tucking her face into my neck. It's drenched within moments by her tears that slide down and soak into the collar of my t-shirt.

One hand just keeps her head pressed there, the other rubs her lower back. My erection fades, and I only think about how I can help to ease Jorie's troubled soul.

Finally, her cries turn to the tiniest of whimpers and finally hiccups. When she takes a stuttering breath and whispers, "I'm okay now," I let her up and roll off the bed. I grab tissues from the bathroom and a bottled water from the mini fridge. After I uncap the water, I hand it to her. I dab at her cheeks as she drinks.

When she's done, she pulls her legs to sit Indian style on the bed and stares blankly at her hands that are folded in her lap.

I sit on the edge of the bed near one of her knees and place my palm there. "Talk to me, Jorie."

She looks up at me with red eyes and a quivering lip. "I'm so confused."

"About me?" I ask her.

"About me," she replies, and this makes me blink in surprise.

Why would she be confused? Jorie is the one who has always known what she wants.

"I don't understand," I say as I squeeze her knee. "But I've got the rest of my life for you to explain it to me."

She studies me for a moment before she says, "I've never loved anyone like I love you."

Fuck… those words.

What they do to me.

Better than any fucking orgasm I've ever had, and that's the God's honest truth.

"But you abandoned me," she continues. "I get you may have been overwhelmed with emotion, or a sense of misplaced priorities to Micah, or even scared shitless over the whole situation. And when it boils down to it, I can love you to the ends of the earth, but you may not be what's best for me."

Christ... if I thought I'd been cut before by the events over the last few weeks, those words right there completely gut me. For the first time, I'm truly afraid of losing Jorie.

"Vince, on the other hand," she says with a watery laugh. "He pulled through for me. He was there when I was at my lowest. He has a lot to atone for, and I don't know if I can make it past the awful things he said and how they made me feel about myself. But he's also offering me something I've always wanted, and that's a committed relationship with children."

My fear skyrockets over those words. Vince brought his fucking A-game to Jorie, except it's not a game at all. I can't judge his intentions because I've not talked to the guy, but whatever he's said... however he's handling things with Jorie, she's truly considering him.

She's fucking considering the man who kicked her out of her home because he's now ready to have babies?

Well, that isn't fucking happening until she knows how I feel about that shit. I get why she's confused now, but she doesn't have all the facts to make a good decision.

"I never thought I wanted kids," I say suddenly, and Jorie sort of jolts at my words. "It wasn't something I really thought about. I was busy building my career, and then Renee and I started dating, getting serious, and then married for all the wrong reasons. Kids never even entered a conversation for us, and when I divorced, I just went on my merry way leading the single life. I never gave my future that kind of thought."

She stares at me transfixed, and I'm not sure she's even breathing, so I continue to get this out.

"Honestly, Jorie... I didn't think about kids when you and I were together either," I say hesitantly, and her lips flatten in disappointment. I forge ahead. "I thought you and I were casual. I thought we had an expiration date. I couldn't see a future with you past what we had planned for the very next day. I thought we had time to figure stuff out, but then the rug got pulled out from underneath us, and suddenly... I didn't have you anymore."

Jorie just continues to watch me silently, but I notice her hands are gripped tight and her knuckles are white.

"You can be damn sure," I tell her as I lean in toward her to look her straight in the eye, "that I've thought of nothing else since your brother came to see me."

"Micah came to see you?" The surprise on her face is evident.

"It's a long story but it involved me punching him and then him helping me pack to come rescue you," I tell her with a small smile.

She gives me one back, and that's something.

"Jorie... I'm suddenly faced now with a woman I love beyond reason who may very well tell me I can't have her. It makes a man put stuff into perspective. It's made me think about what my future really would look like with you in it."

"And what do you think that future would be like?" she asks hesitantly, clearly afraid the answer may not be what she wants to hear.

I squeeze Jorie's knee. "I had intended to do this a lot differently. I thought you'd fall willingly into my arms when you opened that door this morning, and we'd ride off into the sunset together. We'd go back to Vegas and be a couple. I'd propose to you, and it would involve a romantic meal, candles, wine, and bended knee in the restaurant where everyone would watch and clap, and then you would say "yes".

"But instead, I come here to find out you've committed at least a part of yourself to Vince. You came back to him to give the marriage an honest try, and he's brought a lot of promises to your table. But I need you to know I've thought about these things a lot, and my future is with you. As my wife. And as my wife, that means you will have my children. And they have children, and we become grandparents. I know you're confused, but you need to know I'm offering you the same exact thing as Vince. And frankly, our babies would be prettier."

She gives me a hoarse laugh as she reaches out for my hand. "You really want those things with me?"

"Only you," I tell her, my fucking voice breaking from the emotion. "You need to know I'll give you everything you want, but more importantly, you need to know I want it too. Desperately."

"I feel like a contestant on The Dating Game," she finally says bitterly, and the tears well back up in her eyes. "I don't want to hurt Vince, and I don't want to hurt you either."

"Baby," I say soothingly, bringing my hand to her jaw. "The two men in your life both let you down. You'd be a fool not to think through this."

She drops her eyes and nods. "I know."

"But just so you know, I'm not giving up if you choose Vince. I am never going to give up on the hope you'll truly be mine one day. In all ways."

Rubbing her index finger over the back of my hand, she lowers her eyes almost shyly and says, "I told Vince at lunch you were here and that we had sex."

Okay, I fucking want to beat my fists against my chest over that. So sue me.

"How did he take it?" I ask respectfully.

"Not well," she says as she looks back up to me. "I told him that you and I hold an intense connection."

"What we have can't be described, Jorie," I point out, because frankly, this is where I have a leg—or a cock—up on Vince. "What you and I did right there up against the door? That wasn't just sex. That was a joining of souls, and you know I'm right about that."

She nods again, but looks down at where she's holding my hand. I think this is the part where I have to let her fly and hope to fuck she comes back to me.

"Okay," I say as I lean in and give her a quick kiss on

her cheek. Standing, I pull her from the bed. I push her right to the door and open it. "You get out of here and go figure out your shit with Vince."

She turns to me in surprise. "But—"

"But what?" I tease her as I touch the end of my finger to her nose. "You thought you'd just come here and use my body to get your orgasms?"

"I did not think that," she snaps. But then she gives me a guilty look. "But I did think you'd make a move on me."

"See," I tell her with a grin. "I'm full of surprises. And just so you're not tempted to sneak into my room tonight, I'm going to check out and head to the airport, get a flight back out to Vegas."

"You're leaving?" she asks with fear in her eyes.

"I'm giving you space," I correct her. "I'm going to be waiting for you in Vegas. I'm not going to call you or text you, but don't take that to mean I don't want you. On the contrary, I'd like to haul you over my shoulder right now and carry you out of here. But I want you to take the time you need without me influencing your decision."

Her eyes swim with relief. at this point. Things are looking good for me if I was a gambling man, and hey… I own a casino so…

"Jorie…" I lean down to brush my lips against hers. "Don't take forever to figure this out. You've got two of us in limbo."

"I promise," she says with a smile. Her hand goes around my neck, and she kisses me hard. When she pulls back, she says, "I love you. I hope you know that."

"I do," I assure her.

I just hope to fuck it's enough.

CHAPTER 26

Jorie

I DON'T GO home immediately after leaving the hotel. I had honestly thought I would be there a few hours, because given the passion we'd engaged in earlier, I was convinced Walsh wasn't going to let me go until he had me again. Or even again after that.

I'm not sure what it says about me—about the type of woman I am—that I'm disappointed he didn't. I've got two men who want me, one of which I share a home and a marriage certificate with, but I wanted Walsh inside me again. I craved it. Needed it.

I miss it so much.

I instead drive to a small nature park that's a few miles from our neighborhood. I'm not dressed to hike so I merely walk through a small arboretum, looking at the various plants and trees. Taking peace in nature, even as my inner being is fraught with stress and turmoil over what to do.

I mean… I know what to do.

It's Walsh. It can only ever be Walsh.

But there's a small part of me that can't discount the fact I'm married to someone I loved a great deal, and still hold some love for. We'd drifted apart and miscommunicated about key issues. Those things seem to be something we can work on if we wanted to rebuild our future together.

Then there's the pain of heartbreak and how that destroys trust. Vince tore my self-esteem apart and kicked me out. It was selfish and cruel.

Walsh simply abandoned me in favor of my brother's friendship, proving I wasn't good enough for him. My self-esteem took another drastic hit. It was also selfish and cruel.

And yet, both men know they were wrong. They are scrambling to prove it to me, and they are both offering me the world.

They are both offering me exactly what I want.

Taking a seat on a bench under a shade tree, I pull out my phone and call my brother for the first time since he drove Walsh and me apart.

He answers on the first ring. "Jorie… I'm so glad you finally called me. I'm so damn sorry for what I did. I've been so worried about you—"

"Did you send Walsh here?" I ask.

"No," he says outright. "But I did approach him to work things out. I went to him to apologize for what I did, because I had no right to insist you two stay apart.

It's caused so much pain, I can't forgive—"

"I forgive you," I say somewhat irritably because I just don't feel like hearing the apologies anymore. Everyone's damn sorry. Vince is sorry, Walsh is sorry, Micah is sorry. Okay, so that's really three men who have hurt me deeply, and yet… I still love them all in different ways.

Forgiveness is the only option.

"Then why did he really come, Micah?" I ask him softly. "As my brother, tell me why Walsh was here today."

"Because he loves you," he says simply. "You are it for him, Jorie. He made a grave mistake by listening to me rather than his heart, and he knows it."

"So, the things he said to me could be just words to get me back?" I ask, but I know deep down, that's not Walsh. Still, I sort of want to gauge how much Micah and Walsh have made amends with each other.

"He's legit, Jor," he chides. "He loves you. Would take a bullet for you. Will bust his ass every day for the rest of his life to give you anything you could ever desire. And yes, that means those things you hold most important, like a family. He's ready for it, honey. I know it deep in my heart, and I hope you know it, too."

"I'm not sure," I say hesitantly, because there's still one thing that's bothering me. "He told me about Renee."

"Okay," he drawls, not understanding her significance.

"He said they were together and got married because the sex was fantastic and no other reason. Walsh and I have fantastic sex, and that was all it was supposed to be. How do I know that's not all this really is?"

"Outside of the fact I don't ever want to talk to you about your sex life with Walsh, I don't think you're anything like Renee."

"But how do I know that for sure?" I press him. "I don't want to turn my heart back over to Walsh and have him crush it again after a year, when he realizes it was a mistake to marry for sex again."

Micah's silent for a moment, then he becomes absolutely no help whatsoever. "You're going to have to ask him that, Jorie. If it's bothering you, and you need to know… just ask him."

I roll my eyes to the sunny sky above.

"But, Jorie," Micah continues. "I know what you and Walsh have is in a different stratosphere than what he had with Renee. I know this, because even though he pushed you away to appease me, it crushed him. And then it angered him, and he was gladly going to cut me out of his life because of it. It showed me he loved you more than anything in this world."

Well, that's something, I guess, but it still isn't providing me that bright line answer I need.

Or maybe the answer doesn't even lay with Micah and Walsh, but instead lays with Vince.

I let out a sigh of fatigue and tell my brother, "Okay… thanks for the advice."

"What are you going to do?" he asks.

"I'm going to go talk to Vince, then I'm going to take a drive up the coast and be by myself for a while. I'm going to think things through without anyone chattering in my ear, giving me their opinions, or making me promises. I'm going to listen to my heart, but I'm also going to listen to my brain."

"You'll choose Walsh," he says confidently.

"I could choose neither," I reply calmly.

He doesn't have a rejoinder for that, so instead he says, "You'll make the right decision whatever it is. And Jorie?"

"Yeah?"

"I know you say you forgive me, but I'm ashamed I did that to you as your brother. I'll do whatever I can to make it up to you."

"Nothing's needed," I assure him. "I know you were caught off guard. We lied to you. I'm sorry for that as well. There wasn't a good excuse. But next time I see you, I've got to tell you some things about Walsh."

"From when you were younger?" he asks.

"Yes, when I was sixteen, and before you get weirded out, it was nothing sexual at all. But something happened that created a bond between us, and I need to tell you about it because I want you to know why I love him so much. I want you to know that what you saw in the club that night... that was just a small part of who we are. It just goes much deeper, okay?"

"Okay," he says softly, and I can hear the smile on his face. "And for the record, just one more time, let me say you should choose Walsh."

"Goodbye, Micah," I say teasingly.

"I love you," he replies.

"I love you," I tell him before I hang up.

I don't dally in the arboretum, but make my way back to the house. I consider stopping by the grocery store to make something for dinner, but that smacks of a domesticity I'm not feeling, especially since Vince and I are going to have to talk tonight. I doubt I'll be able to eat I'm so wrought with emotions over this.

I park my car in the driveway and walk up to the house I've shared with my husband. It's the same one he kicked me out of over a month ago.

Part of me is ashamed I've come back.

Part of me knows it was the right decision at the time, given all I was faced with.

I don't know that I'll ever reconcile those in my mind, so I am going to choose to let that go. Besides, in the grand scheme of things, what's done is done and I need to look forward.

As I walk up the porch, I pull my keys out of my purse. Before I can even reach the door, Vince is there swinging it open. I can tell he's relieved to see me, and it makes me feel so guilty.

Perhaps it was an unwise decision to come back.

"What are you doing here?" I ask in surprise as I push my keys back in my purse. Vince doesn't usually get home from work until close to seven.

"I canceled my appointments for the rest of the day," he says as he steps back, pulling the door open wider so I can walk in. "Thought it was more important that we talk."

I nod as I walk by, pausing to put my hand on his chest as I look up at him. "Thank you. I'd like to talk, too."

I choose the living room, and Vince follows me. Putting my purse down on a side table, I take an end on the couch. Vince chooses an adjacent chair, and when he's settled, I pull my legs underneath me.

We stare at each other a moment, and then he asks, "Did you sleep with him again?"

"No," I say with quiet empathy to how this must make him feel. "We just talked."

"You said you needed to tell me things about Walsh. About your history with him."

"Yes. But first, I need to tell you that I don't have a decision made right now. I know what my heart is telling me, but it's been so battered lately, I don't know if I should trust it. I want to tell you everything—and some of it's not going to be easy for you to hear—and then I want you to tell me what you want from me."

"Okay," he returns as he leans back in the chair to

watch me warily.

"I don't need to tell you how badly you hurt me," I start by saying. "But when you had me leave our home, I left believing that I wasn't worthy of a man. You made me doubt myself and my sexuality."

"I'm sorry—"

"Don't," I say gently as I hold my hand up. "You've apologized already, and you explained what drove you to say that. I get it. I just need you to know what my frame of mind was when I left, and why it led me to Walsh."

Vince's jaw tightens in anticipation of whatever boom I'm getting to lower on him. I decide to just rip the Band-Aid off.

"I went to a sex club with Elena," I say, then I wait to see his reaction.

He grimaces and lets out a rush of air as his gaze darts to the fireplace where he just stares at it blankly.

"It was a masquerade event, so everyone's faces were covered. Walsh was there and we had sex, not knowing at first who the other person was."

Vince turns back to me, clearly distressed by learning his wife went to a sex club because he'd made her feel like shit. "I'm so sorry, Jorie. I didn't mean to drive you to that."

I shake my head rapidly. "I don't want you to be sorry for that. That experience... and then later with Walsh... it gave me back my dignity, believe it or not. And I don't say that to hurt you, but I need you to know it served a very good purpose for me."

"And led you to Walsh," he says somewhat bitterly.

"I'm not telling you these details to hurt you, but rather to explain my history with Walsh," I tell him gently. He nods, and I go on. "During that encounter, my breasts were bared and Walsh saw my scars."

"The ones you got from that car accident?" he asks, because that's what I've told anyone in my life who have ever seen them.

I shake my head. "They weren't from a car accident. I was attacked and almost raped when I was sixteen. It was in a fancy hotel bathroom where a high school party was going on. As I was fighting them off—"

"Them?" he croaks in horror.

"There were two of them," I explain. "And I was fighting them so hard, a huge glass vase got knocked over and a long sharp piece went through my breast. The boys freaked out and ran. Micah and my dad were out of town, so I called Walsh."

"That's how he recognized you in the club?" he guesses.

"Yes, but that's not what's important about that story. Walsh carried me out of that glass, got me an ambulance, and rode to the hospital with me. He was by my side as they stitched me up. I didn't want to involve the police, and Walsh respected my decision not to do so."

"But why?" he asks with his eyebrows drawn deeply

together.

"Because I was drunk. Because I shouldn't have been there. Because I wasn't raped, and because those boys went to my school, and I didn't want it to be public. There were many reasons taken all together; I just didn't want to deal with it that way."

Vince nods with what looks like understanding.

"Walsh kept my secret all these years," I tell him. "He promised not to tell Micah or my dad. He stood by my side and was the only one who knew of my trauma, although later, I told Elena. But more than that, Walsh exacted vengeance for me. He promised to keep my secret in exchange for their names, and while Walsh thought I gave their names up reluctantly, the truth is I gave them to him without a second thought. I knew he would hurt them, and Vince… he really, really hurt them."

"He was your champion," he murmurs in understanding.

"Even before that. For much of my life, he did things that made him my champion. Same as Micah, in a big brother sort of way, but Walsh and I have a bond that most people don't share because of that one incident."

"Add sex into the mixture, and it was easy to fall in love with him," he says dejectedly.

"No," I correct him. "It wasn't easy to fall in love with him. I told you… our sexual chemistry is almost surreal. But at first, that's all it was. That's all I ever thought it would be, and I took it. I took what he offered, and we kept another secret. We didn't tell Micah about this because a few years back, Micah had told Walsh I was off limits to him. Walsh was respecting those limits."

"And Micah found out?"

"Yes, and he told Walsh to stay out of my life, and so he did," I tell him with a tinge of remaining bitterness in my voice at Walsh's betrayal. "He chose Micah."

"That was a douche thing to do if he loved you," Vince points out, striking quickly to make sure I don't forget the way Walsh hurt me.

"It devastated me, Vince," I tell him truthfully. "The pain of that is still fresh to me even now. It's why when you came to me, it wasn't hard for me to accept your offer to come back to L.A. I was depressed and couldn't see any happiness for me. I latched on to you and your promises for a fresh start, really hoping you and I could perhaps make something of the tatters."

"And I meant every word I said to you," he affirms. "There weren't ulterior motives."

"I know that," I assure him.

"I guess what I don't understand," Vince says, "both of us hurt you, but Jorie… you clearly love Walsh. You don't love me like the way you love him. It seems to me your decision should be easy."

I shake my head. "It's not. My trust is a little bruised. And Walsh was married before, and it was all about the great sex. I'm not sure I can trust that what we have is more than that."

Vince just does that slow blink thing where I know I said something stupid.

"What?" I ask.

"You just told me that you and Walsh have a bond that's unlike any other probably in your life," Vince points out. "I hate to even give the guy any credit, but Jorie... he made a mistake and didn't choose you. It doesn't mean his feelings weren't real or deep. If he loves you the way you love him—I can't compete with that. I guess I don't know why you're not choosing him."

"I don't know," I whisper. "I don't know why I'm so afraid."

"You need to decide what to do."

"I don't have to decide right now," I tell him. "But I do have to make the right decision."

"What is Walsh offering you?" he asks me bluntly.

I hesitate a moment, my throat constricting as if I'm almost afraid to believe what Walsh told me. "Everything," I whisper. "He's offering me everything."

CHAPTER 27

Walsh

I PULL MY meal out of the microwave—some prepackaged frozen lasagna my housekeeper keeps stocked for late-night hunger emergencies—as I talk to Micah on the cell phone pressed between my ear and shoulder. He returned to San Francisco today. Some steam escapes out of the corner of container and catches me on my thumb.

"Ouch, fuck," I yell as I drop the thing on the counter and bobble the phone. I mutter, "Hang on."

I put the phone on the counter, hit the speaker phone button, and say, "Can you hear me okay?"

"Yeah," he says. "You were telling me how you left it off with Jorie."

Indeed, I was. I called Micah about the trip I just got back from about four hours ago. I came straight home and had been catching up on some work at my kitchen table. It's only when I looked at the clock and saw it was almost ten did I realize I hadn't eaten lunch or dinner and I was suddenly starved.

Now it's a microwave meal and probably some *Sons of Anarchy* to cap my evening off. Besides, it will help keep my mind off Jorie.

"We talked," I tell Micah. I absolutely don't tell him about fucking her against the door. "And it was good, I think. She's confused, and there's Vince, of course."

"She'll choose you," Micah says confidently.

"I want her to choose what's best," I return as I peel the plastic cover off the lasagna. "I hope to fuck that's me, but it has to be what's best for her."

"You're best," Micah says again.

"Just two weeks ago, you were not keen on this idea," I remind him.

"And you punched me hard and knocked some sense into me," he says with a laugh, and I can't help but join him. It's like all the bad shit was quickly melting away between us.

"I talked to her today," Micah says. "She called me after she talked to you."

"What did she say?" I ask with great interest. Especially if it eases my mind a bit.

"That's between me and her, but I was vocal that I thought you were the real deal."

"Gee, thanks," I mutter. "I've been telling her the same thing."

"There is an issue though that's bothering her," Micah says, and my heart drops. How can there be an issue? I thought I covered everything I knew was important to her.

"Come on, man," I say with a groan. "Don't do this to me."

"That's for her to bring it up, because maybe it's ultimately not an issue for her. But I told her she had to talk about it to you."

A surge of irritation sweeps through me, and I snap, "Well, that could be days—even weeks—Micah. What am I supposed to do until then? Steal my secretary's Xanax from her desk drawer?"

Just then, my elevator doors hiss open and I blink my eyes.

Jorie is standing there.

She's got on a pair of faded jeans, a fitted t-shirt, and flip-flops. Over one shoulder is her purse, and her other hand has a rolling suitcase.

"Your sister's here. Gotta go," I lean down to mutter into the speaker, and I disconnect Micah.

When I look back up at her, she's moved out of the elevator but hasn't come in any further. I stay behind the kitchen island facing her, afraid if I blink, she'll only be an apparition.

"What are you doing here?" I ask her, completely befuddled to see her. Not that I'm not fucking over the moon about it, but by my accounts, she should be deep in conversation with Vince about now.

"It's you," she murmurs, and my heart comes to a stuttering halt. "It's only ever going to be you."

Inside, I'm doing a fist pump but on the outside, I'm rounding the kitchen island with long strides. I practically knock her over when I crash into her, hands in that beautiful hair and my mouth fusing to hers. Jorie drops her purse, and I vaguely hear her suitcase fall over. Her arms wrap tight around me. What I'm getting from her is that she's never letting me go.

Thank fuck.

Finally, I pull my mouth of hers, but I keep my face close so I can look at her in wonder. "How? Why?"

She opens her mouth, but I kiss her again instead. When I pull back, I mutter as I take her by the hand. "No, wait… don't tell me. I have something else to do first."

I pull her toward the kitchen, and Jorie laughs. "Figured it would take you ten seconds to drag me off to bed."

I grin but come to a halt by the kitchen table, pushing her down into a chair. "Not taking you to bed yet."

"Huh?"

"Don't move," is all I say.

She watches me in silence as I bustle around the kitchen. First, I pull out a plate, cutlery, and a wineglass. I set them on the table in front of her. I grab wine from the fridge, pour her a glass. Sneaking a glance at her, I can see amused curiosity on her face.

Lastly, I take my microwaved lasagna that's a little burned on the edges, and I turn it over to dump it on the plate.

Jorie snickers.

"Just a few more things," I tell her as I search through my cabinets and finally find a pair candlestick holders with candles in there. I think they were Renee's, but I sure as fuck know I've never used them. I forage through a drawer and find matches.

I set the candles on the table and light them.

"I'm not hungry, Walsh," she says with a laugh.

"Be quiet," I chastise her with a mock glare. "I need one more thing… don't move."

I run into the hallway that leads off the kitchen, to my duffle bag on the bed, and dig my hand down inside. I'd carried this with me to Los Angeles, but I never brought it out.

It wasn't the right time then.

I jog back into the kitchen and slide to a halt right beside Jorie's chair. She looks up at me with raised eyebrows, the ring box securely hidden in my hand.

"What's all this?" she asks.

"Well," I say dramatically as I get down on one knee in front of her. At my obvious movement, a hand comes up to cover her mouth in surprise. "Remember in Los Angeles earlier today, I told you I wanted you to be my wife, and I envisioned us at a romantic restaurant when I proposed on bended knee? I can't conjure that up right now, and I don't want to wait another fucking second. I don't know how you came to the decision you did, but you're here and I'm asking you to marry me right now."

Jorie gasps as I open my hand to present the black velvet box to her.

She stares at it with wide eyes, so I go ahead and open it.

Another gasp and her eyes go even more wide. I outdid myself yesterday when I picked this out before I went to the airport to fly to L.A. It's a Harry Winston, four-carat behemoth sapphire in a classic emerald cut. It's flanked by trilliant diamonds on the side, each a full carat, set in white gold.

"Holy shit, Walsh," she wheezes as she looks from the ring to me. "You're totally compensating."

I smirk at her and pull the ring out. Taking her left hand, I slide it on the finger that will proclaim that this woman is off the market.

She stares at it in wonder and says, "You know I'm still married, right?"

"Semantics," I say dismissively, but we are going to work on that divorce thing as soon as possible.

Sliding her gaze back up to me she whispers, "Do you want your answer?"

I smile at her, lean in to kiss her mouth. "I had my answer the minute you walked into my home with your suitcase. But I'd love to hear it from that gorgeous mouth."

"It's yes," she says with a little bit of an excited squeal, and it's music to my ears.

I kiss her again hard, then I'm lifting her from the chair. She wraps her legs around my waist, her arms tight around my neck, and she doesn't move her lips from mine until I toss her down on my bed.

"I take it by the change of clothes when I saw you after lunch, you took a shower?" I ask as I peel her jeans and panties down her legs. She's working on tearing her t-shirt off.

"Yeah, why?" she returns breathlessly as she comes to her knees and helps me with my clothes as I stand at the edge of the bed.

She leans in, runs her tongue over one of my nipples after my shirt comes off, and I hiss from the touch. My hands shoot out, take her face, and I pull her up closer to me. "I was hoping you hadn't showered. I wanted to see my cum dried white on the inside of your thighs."

"So freaking dirty." She laughs, and I kiss her hard as she works at my belt.

When my pants are off, our naked bodies hit the bed and we do nothing but kiss, fondle, and touch hidden places. None of it with the goal to get each other off, but merely to build each other up.

Finally, when Jorie says, "I need you now, Walsh," I surge up her body and slide into her heat.

Fucking perfect.

MUCH LATER, WHEN we've had our immediate fill, I sit

on the bed with my back against the headboard. Jorie straddles my lap as she studies the ring on her finger. My hands slide up and down her thighs lazily. I'm mellow, sated, and fucking in love with my soon-to-be wife.

Soon as the divorce papers are finalized for her and Vince, that is.

"When did you get this?" she asks curiously.

"Stopped on the way to the airport yesterday," I tell her. "I had every intention of proposing to you there. Almost whipped it out after I fucked you, but that didn't seem very romantic. But then after we talked at the hotel, I knew it wasn't the right time. You didn't need that pressure on you."

Jorie brings her gaze from the ring to me and places her hands on my shoulders. "I'm sorry you had to wait for me to make a choice."

"You didn't make me wait long," I say dryly, but with gratitude. I was expecting a few days at least. "Which, by the way, what happened after you left the hotel?"

"I stopped at a local park, and did some thinking. I called Micah. Then I went home and I was surprised to find Vince there. He had taken the afternoon off and wanted to be there when I got home so we could go ahead and talk. He didn't want it to drag out."

"And the talk went well?" I ask tentatively, not wanting to get all up in her business, but more curious than ever as to how she came to her decision.

"Vince was the one who talked me into coming here tonight," she tells me, her eyes twinkling with amusement.

"Vince?"

She nods. "I told him all about our history together growing up. That night in the hotel bathroom. How you made me feel about myself as a woman after I'd been brought so low. I told him how crushed I was when you walked away from me, and well… he just could see it clear as day where I probably couldn't. I told him I needed some time to think, but he just came right back at me and told me it was clear I didn't. He told me I was meant to be with you and that I needed to not keep you waiting."

"Jesus," I breathe out in astonishment. I owe this fucking dude big time. Maybe I'll invite him to our wedding. But I don't say any of those things, because I want to be respectful. "Is he okay?"

Jorie's eyes get a light sheen of sadness, but she nods. "He will be."

"And just like that, you accepted his word that I was right for you?" I ask, because nothing Jorie's said so far tells me that she knows that deep in her heart. She's only said yes to my proposal.

"What did I say when I stepped out of the elevator?" she asks me.

My mind blanks. I try to remember, but I was so fucking overwhelmed at seeing her there, I can't for the life of me remember just now.

"I told you, Walsh," she says softly, leaning in to brush her lips against mine. "I said it was *you*. It was *only* ever you."

"Now it's only ever us," I tell her.

"Vince said he'd file for divorce soon," she says, and that takes a weight off me. "It can be finalized six months after that."

"So we should plan for a wedding in maybe seven months, then?" I ask with a grin.

"If you want," she says quietly. "But I don't want anything big. We can go to a chapel here or something."

"We are not fucking getting married by Elvis," I mutter. "Maybe a destination wedding?"

"Can Micah come?" she asks.

"I suppose," I hedge, as if I'm still pissed at her brother, but frankly… Jorie on my lap wearing my ring? I can't be pissed about anything.

"I love you," she says softly and then leans her entire torso against mine, so I can wrap her up in a hug. She lays her head on my shoulder, tightens her arms around my neck. I squeeze her close to me and tell her, "I love you too, Jorie. Always have."

We stay that way, pressed into one another as we cherish the fact we are starting a new life as of right now.

But then I'm a dude, and did I mention I've been two weeks without this woman, so I ask her, "Any way I could possibly get a hand job with that ring hand? I'd like to see that puppy moving up and down my cock."

Jorie bursts out laughing as she leans back to look at me. "You make me so happy, Walsh."

"Going to make you happier each day," I promise.

"Damn right you are," she quips as she moves off my lap and takes my dick in her hand.

The sapphire looks stunning as the starts to stroke me up and down.

EPILOGUE

Jorie

"Mrs. Brooks," Walsh groans as he licks between my legs. "You taste so much better as my wife."

I want to giggle, but I let out a long moan instead as he pulls my clit through his lips to suck on it. A hand snakes up my belly to palm my breast, before he starts pinching a nipple. That is somehow connected directly to my pussy because it immediately tightens, contracts, and then I explode with a scream that I cut short because we're in an elegant Parisian hotel and I don't want to be crass.

Walsh chuckles as he licks me down off my high, and when I'm breathing normally again, he surprises me by pulling me off the bed.

"Wait," I say as I pull back against him. "You need to consummate this marriage, like right now."

Walsh laughs and pulls me off the bed harder, so I have no choice but to go. He laughs, because technically, we got married three days ago, and we sure as hell already consummated. We chose to just get our license at the courthouse with Micah and Elena in attendance, and then we boarded a private jet to Paris for a two-week honeymoon.

Of course, Walsh being Walsh, as soon as the bellman left our room, he had me naked in like two seconds flat.

"Let's check out our view," he says as he pulls me to the window. Our hotel supposedly has amazing views of the Eiffel Tower and knowing Walsh, he paid for the best available.

When he throws the curtains back, I just blink at the building that's next to us completely blocking any view of the tower.

"Oh," I say in disappointment. "Maybe they made a mistake in the reservation."

Walsh pulls me in front of him, pushes me closer to the window, and steps up behind me so I can feel his erection at my backside. "Look closer, baby."

And so I focus on the building that seems just feet away, and heat flushes through my body as I realize it's some type of apartment building. It has the same elegant gray stone architecture of the building we're in, and it looks insanely high end.

But more importantly, most of the windows are completely transparent, looking straight into people's homes. Since it's in the middle of the day, most blinds and windows are open. While there aren't many people moving around in the various dwellings we can see from our hotel window, my first instinct is to move back from ours as I'm completely stark ass naked.

"Relax, Mrs. Brooks," Walsh leans over to whisper in my ear. "This is a city of love and romance. I bet any one of those people wouldn't mind watching some horny honeymooners getting it on, don't you think?"

"Oh, God," I groan as my head falls back onto his chest.

"One of my wedding presents to you," Walsh whispers. "You wanted to fuck where people could see us."

I was absolutely drenched from what Walsh just did to me, but now my pussy is contracting with need. Walsh slips a hand around my stomach and brings it down between my legs. He pushes us right up to the window, and my palms go out to rest against the cool glass.

"Anyone watching?" he asks as his lips go to my neck and his fingers dip inside me.

My eyes scan the various open apartments, and I see a man reading his newspaper by the window while he drinks perhaps a cup of coffee. Two over and one floor up, a woman is exercising by her window. My eyes roam around, and there's a man a few floors up standing at his window, talking on his phone while he looks out. He's got a hand casually tucked in his pocket as he looks down at the city street below.

And then, his gaze slides up, moves past us, and then slams back onto the scene we're putting on.

"Man watching us," I gasp as Walsh starts rubbing my clit. My hips buck not only from the sensation, but because the man is now watching us hungrily. He says something into the phone and then disconnects it. When he leans against the window with his forearm pressed into the glass above his head, his hand starts moving in his pocket.

"He's turned on," I whisper as Walsh strums between my legs. "He's touching himself in his pocket."

"Pinch your nipples for him," Walsh says, his mouth still lightly grazing my neck, not even bothering to look up at the guy. I do as he asks, my gaze never leaving the man watching me across the way.

Then his hand is out of his pocket and working at his belt. He efficiently takes his dick out, and it looks very nice from where I am. It's thick and hard, and he crudely spits in his hand to give himself some lube. The action is so dirty, and it's so perverted that he's getting off on me getting off, that an orgasm takes me by surprise. My back arches so my body presses into the glass, and my eyes close tight for a few seconds, while pleasure wracks my body.

"Fucking beautiful," Walsh murmurs, and my eyes slide open, immediately locking on the man still jacking off, although his strokes have slowed down a bit too, perhaps to wait for us to start up again. He gives me a wicked smile as he masturbates.

"Fuck me, baby," I tell Walsh as I reach a hand back and take his dick in a hard squeeze.

"As my wife demands," Walsh says, and then he steps away for a moment. Then because I feel dirty as hell, I slip my hand down between my legs and lightly stroke my clit, but it's so sensitive it almost hurts. The man in the other building appreciates this and throws me a devilish grin.

Walsh is back, and he's pulled a chair to the window. He turns me so my body is parallel to the window and pushes me over the back of it. I hold onto the top edge and spread my legs as Walsh comes to stand behind me.

I watch the man in the window, who is now watching us both hungrily. His hand is moving a little faster and he's twisting at the top. I hear the snick of a lube bottle opening, and I don't even startle because I very much like that sound. Walsh owns my ass lock, stock, and barrel and I love his cock there.

My husband squirts some cool gel in between my ass cheeks, moving me slightly so the guy jacking off can get an unobstructed view of what Walsh is getting ready to do.

But the guy knows. He started stroking faster when he saw Walsh lubing me up.

Then I feel the fat head of Walsh's cock at my backside, and he's gently pushing the tip in. When it breaches the tight ring of muscle, he's able to slide all the way in with one push.

The masturbating guy's eyes go wide at my ability to handle that, and then I have to forget about him a moment as Walsh starts to fuck my ass. He's putting on a show too. Because he knows I can handle it, he sets up a very fast pace.

My back arches and I toss my head in ecstasy as I take a moment to feel my husband's dick work in and out of me. I push my hand between my legs and play with myself, and when I'm able to handle the rhythm, I turn to watch the guy jacking off. He's tugging on his cock hard, breathing heavily as he watches us. I slide my gaze back to the other windows, and while the one guy still has his nose buried in a newspaper, apparently the woman who was exercising has stopped not only to watch, but she's also called two of her friends to the window.

It appears we've got a crowd.

Walsh groans and grunts, now giving me quite a pounding because he's turned on as hell that people are watching.

"Going to come, Jor," he growls as he plows into me.

And then with a bark, he pulls out of me and comes all over my back and ass. The minute the first warm splash hits my skin, I climax with him. My head drops down. I groan as Walsh pushes his cock back in my ass, where he just slowly moves back and forth while his fingers spread his semen around my skin. I close my eyes and sigh with contentment. I have no clue if the guy across the way came, but I'm going to assume he did.

It doesn't matter to me though, because my husband is then pulling out of me and drawing the curtains closed. He picks me up, carries me to the bathroom, and starts to run us a bath.

I lean back against the vanity and just take a moment to admire the hard planes of his back, and his hair that's still way too long for a businessman, but I love it so much.

As if he senses I'm staring, he looks over his shoulder at me with a smile. "Like that?"

"Mmm-hmm," I acknowledge with a purr. "That was hot."

Walsh tests the water, adds some bath salts, and then stands up. He pulls me into him while we wait for the bath to fill up.

"When do you want to start making babies?" he asks casually, and it startles me so much, my head flies up and I hit him in the chin.

"Ouch," I exclaim.

At the same time, he says, "Shit."

We pull apart and stare at each other as we rub our respective bumps.

"Babies?" I ask in astonishment. "We just got married."

"But we've known each other our entire lives," he points out. "And babies aren't going to change anything."

"Says the man who doesn't have to get fat and squirt a bowling ball out the end of his dick," I say pointedly.

"God… I can't wait for you to get a big tummy," he says, pulling me back to him. "I'm going to fuck you morning, noon, and night."

"Oh, stop it," I chastise him, although that sounds nice.

"You really want to start?" I ask him, and his eyes sober at my question.

"I do, Jorie," he says simply. "If you're ready."

"I'm ready," I say quickly, and then I break out into a smile that feels like it might break my face as I squeal. "Oh, my God… we're going to have kids."

"Excited?" he asks with a laugh.

I pull away from him, rummage through one of my small bags on the vanity, and I pull out my birth control pills. I make a very ceremonious event of pushing each one out of the packet into the toilet before flushing them down.

"I have to say, Mrs. Brooks," Walsh says with a twinkle in his eyes. "The thought of this turns me on so much, I doubt we're going to get much sightseeing done while we're here."

Laughing, I toss the empty pill case in the trash and step back into my husband's body. Laying my cheek on his chest, I tell him, "And I'm completely fine with that, Mr. Brooks."

Thank you for visiting The Wicked Horse! If you enjoyed reading *Wicked Wish* as much as I enjoyed writing it, please consider leaving a review.

The seduction continues at The Wicked Horse Vegas with *Wicked Envy (Wicked Horse Vegas, Book #3)*!

Pre-order Wicked Envy now!

Business at The Wicked Horse Vegas is booming, and everyone in Sin City is lining up to visit the hottest club in Nevada. Whether you're visiting for the day or are a full-fledged member, The Wicked Horse Vegas promises to fulfill your darkest desires, while leaving you with your greatest pleasures. Stop by and visit The Wicked Horse Vegas with the release of *Wicked Envy*, coming October 27, 2017!

Connect with Sawyer online:

Website: sawyerbennett.com

Twitter: www.twitter.com/bennettbooks

Facebook: www.facebook.com/bennettbooks

To see Other Works by Sawyer Bennett, please visit her Book Page on her website.

About the Author

Since the release of her debut contemporary romance novel, Off Sides, in January 2013, Sawyer Bennett has released more than 30 books and has been featured on both the USA Today and New York Times bestseller lists on multiple occasions.

A reformed trial lawyer from North Carolina, Sawyer uses real life experience to create relatable, sexy stories that appeal to a wide array of readers. From new adult to erotic contemporary romance, Sawyer writes something for just about everyone.

Sawyer likes her Bloody Marys strong, her martinis dirty, and her heroes a combination of the two. When not bringing fictional romance to life, Sawyer is a chauffeur, stylist, chef, maid, and personal assistant to a very active toddler, as well as full-time servant to two adorably naughty dogs. She believes in the good of others, and that a bad day can be cured with a great work-out, cake, or a combination of the two.

Made in the USA
Lexington, KY
19 August 2017